"Talk to me," L... hear your voic... you are."

"What would you like... of acid in her tone.

"How about 'Thanks, Lucas. You've just spent a day of your life trying to keep me safe and I really appreciate it.' That would be nice for starters."

"Dream on." But she did thank him, even if she couldn't bring herself to verbally express it. "Look, I feel bad...I didn't want to involve you."

"And what is it that you think I want to do?"

Irritation made his voice rough, and she responded with a hint of heat. "If those men are as dangerous as you say, then I didn't want to put you...I wanted to fix this myself."

"Lady, you may be a great photographer, but as a strategist against mobsters and murderers, you need some training."

She jerked her blouse over her head. And just in time. He turned around as she pulled her hair free from her collar. His normally blue eyes were a gunmetal gray, and the intensity of his look made her catch her breath. He was furious with her, but it didn't stop the heart-stopping jolt that ran through her body. Dealing with Lucas West was like grabbing a tornado and trying to hang on.

25 years of INTRIGUE

Dear Harlequin Intrigue Reader,

In honor of two very special events, the Harlequin Intrigue editorial team has planned exceptional promotions to celebrate throughout 2009. To kick off the year, we're celebrating Harlequin Books' 60th Diamond Anniversary with DIAMONDS AND DADDIES, an exciting four-book miniseries featuring protective dads and their extraordinary proposals to four very lucky women. Rita Herron launches the series with *Platinum Cowboy* next month.

Later in the year Harlequin Intrigue celebrates its own 25th anniversary. To mark the event we've asked reader favorites to return with their most popular series.

• Debra Webb has created a new COLBY AGENCY trilogy. This time out, Victoria Colby-Camp will need to enlist the help of her entire staff of agents for her own family crisis.

• You can return to 43 LIGHT STREET with Rebecca York and join Caroline Burnes on another crime-solving mission with Familiar the Black Cat Detective.

• Next stop: WHITEHORSE, MONTANA with B.J. Daniels for more Big Sky mysteries with a new family. Meet the Corbetts—Shane, Jud, Dalton, Lantry and Russell.

Because we know our readers love following trace evidence, we've created the new continuity KENNER COUNTY CRIME UNIT. Whether collecting evidence or tracking down leads, lawmen and investigators have more than their jobs on the line, because the real mystery is one of the heart. Pick up *Secrets in Four Corners* by Debra Webb this month, and don't miss any one of the terrific stories to follow in this series.

And that's just a small selection of what we have planned to thank our readers.

We'd love to hear from you, and hope you enjoy all of our special promotions this year.

Happy reading, and happy anniversary, Harlequin Books!

Sincerely,

Denise Zaza
Senior Editor
Harlequin Intrigue

CAROLINE BURNES

FAMILIAR VOWS

HARLEQUIN®

TORONTO • NEW YORK • LONDON
AMSTERDAM • PARIS • SYDNEY • HAMBURG
STOCKHOLM • ATHENS • TOKYO • MILAN • MADRID
PRAGUE • WARSAW • BUDAPEST • AUCKLAND

For Kim Robertson, cat lover and Familiar fan

Recycling programs
for this product may
not exist in your area.

ISBN-13: 978-0-373-88881-8
ISBN-10:   0-373-88881-3

FAMILIAR VOWS

Copyright © 2009 by Carolyn Haines

www.eHarlequin.com

Printed in U.S.A.

ABOUT THE AUTHOR

Caroline Burnes has published more than forty Harlequin Intrigue books, many of them featuring Familiar, the Black Cat Detective. She first published with the Intrigue line in 1988 with a book called *A Deadly Breed*. Since that time, many of her stories have featured animals: horses, cats, dogs and even a few wolves and cougars thrown in for good measure. She lives on a farm in South Alabama with seven horses, eight cats and six dogs, most of them rescue animals. She urges everyone to please spay and neuter their companion pets to help reduce the number of unwanted animals.

Books by Caroline Burnes

CAST OF CHARACTERS

Michelle Sieck—She has a talent for taking extraordinary photographs—and for getting into trouble. When she snaps a wedding without permission, she sets in motion events that threaten innocent people, herself included.

Lucas West—A man scarred by the murder of his brother, Lucas wants justice. And he wants to protect the chief witness who testified against his brother's killer. Michelle is a thorn in his flesh and a fire in his heart.

Familiar—Smart, savvy and always ready for a good case, Familiar finds himself in the backwoods of Alabama in his efforts to protect headstrong Michelle—and to help find the missing witness, Lorry.

Lorry Kennedy (aka Anna Sewell)—Lorry was at the wrong place at the wrong time. She witnessed a brutal hit on an undercover cop, and she was brave enough to testify. But as Antonio Maxim's case comes up for appeal, Lorry is a prime target.

Antonio Maxim—Antonio heads a crime organization that spreads from Texas to New York City and involves luring innocent young girls into "modeling" jobs which turn out to be forced prostitution and drug running. He's in jail—but can Lucas and Michelle keep him there?

Robert Maxim—Antonio's brother, Robert is moving up in the ranks of the criminal world. He has one chance to free his brother, and that involves killing Lorry Kennedy or anyone who gets in his way.

Chapter One

Ah, back in the South, where food is an art form and no humanoid would ever dare mention that I'm back at the hors d'oeuvres table for the fourth time. Love those salmon puffs in dill sauce! The yellowfin-tuna croquettes are superb. Let the bipeds waste their caloric allowance on champagne; I'm indulging in sustenance that will make my coat sleek and shiny and my eyes bright. Brain food, yum!

Everyone is taking their seats. The harpist has started. I do believe it's showtime. And I've got to scurry to get to my seat beside my beloved owner, Eleanor.

I have to say, the bride is beautiful. The entire theme of a Civil War wedding, while admittedly strange to a feline, is beautiful. Charles looks handsome in his uniform, with the sword at his side and the gold sash, and Lorry is magnificent in a hand-stitched gown crusted with seed pearls. Maybe it's just pretend, but the bridal party's attire gives the wedding a solemnity that makes me believe Charles and Lorry will truly find happiness together. From what Eleanor tells me, Lorry deserves a break. Her life hasn't been easy.

Ah, the bridesmaids have assumed their places, and all eyes turn to watch Lorry float down the aisle like a dream.

Uh-oh. It looks like the tall, lean best man has seen something he doesn't particularly care for. It almost looks as if he's going to bolt from his place, but no, he can't, or the ceremony will be ruined.

But what does Lucas West see? All afternoon he stalked the wedding, as if he expected Jack the Ripper to show up, and now he's craning his neck to watch…a woman with a camera? She's probably been paid to assist the guy who's photographing the wedding. Why should that unsettle Lucas so much? Two photogs instead of one—not cause for alarm as far as I can tell.

I have to say, though, the woman shutterbug should be in front of the camera, not behind it. She's simply beautiful, and she has no clue. She's all about getting her shot. And the money shot is the bride.

Lorry, with her honey-gold hair and inner

*beauty, is glowing with happiness. Miss Shut-
terbug is following her with studied diligence.
Camera Girl is intense, that's for sure. She's
going to get her picture, and the world be
damned. She even stepped in front of the other
photographer, which didn't go over well with
him or with Lucas.*

*Now Lucas and Eleanor are both acting
strange. I'm sure there's a story behind this,
and I'll find out as soon as the vows are said.*

THE LIGHTING in the old clapboard church was
incredible. Michelle moved around the chapel,
her cameras whirring as she recorded the
wedding digitally and also on film. Of the four
weddings she'd photographed so far on this
assignment for *Bride Magazine,* this one was
the best—at least photographically speaking.
The magazine had offered florists across the
nation a free ad for alerting the magazine to the
most unusual wedding, and Michelle made a
mental note to send Bloomers Unlimited a
thank-you note. This wedding was fantastic.

She had no clue if the bride and groom loved
each other or had a chance at "happily ever
after." The truth was, she didn't care. What
mattered was capturing the image—that
perfect blend of light, composition and human
emotion, where one picture told the entire story.

As she moved along the west wall of the church, flanking the bride, Michelle noticed the best man giving her the evil eye. In fact, he looked as if he was going to step out of his role as Confederate attendant to the groom and confront her. Had she not been so focused on her work, she might have found that idea a tiny bit thrilling. He was the antithesis of the men she knew in New York. He was rugged and self-contained, and for some reason, she thought of the old black-and-white reruns of Marshal Dillon on *Gunsmoke*. Too bad he was eyeing her like she was a horse thief he meant to hang.

She tried to ignore him, but his steely gaze made her uncomfortable. Yes, she was an inter-loper at this wedding. What she offered this soon-to-be wife was something most brides would kill for—a featured photo essay in *Bride Magazine*.

Michelle used only natural light, so the flash wasn't an issue during the ceremony. Yet when she caught a glimpse beneath the bride's veil, she saw a young woman clearly in despair. It made Michelle uneasy, but she continued to do her job. Heck, if Iggy Adams, her editor-in-chief, couldn't talk the couple into signing a release to use the photos, they wouldn't be used. No one wanted a lawsuit.

When the groom lifted the veil, the purest light filtered in through a loft window, and Michelle snapped a photo that every photographer waits a lifetime to get. The groom bent to kiss the bride, and then it was over.

Michelle sighed, wishing she actually knew this couple. But she'd never met them. As part of the deal she'd cut with Iggy, she had no responsibility to inform the bride and groom about the photographs. The whole idea of catching the bride and groom unaware—while it had yielded some of the best wedding photographs she'd ever seen—was still a bit strange. But that was Iggy's problem. All she had to do was show up and get the pictures. Iggy would handle the sticky details.

Speaking of moving on down the road, she had another wedding to shoot. It was time to book out.

She picked up her camera bag and took long strides toward the exit, almost stumbling over a black cat, who stared up at her as if he had something to say.

"Hey, kitty." She bent to stroke his sleek fur, but his gaze never wavered. He watched her. Not critically, but with curiosity. Well, she'd always heard that curiosity killed the cat. Too bad she didn't have a way to take this black beauty home with her to the Big Apple. He had the attitude and demeanor of the perfect roommate.

When she walked outside, she was amused to see that the cat followed her. Maybe he didn't have a home. She gave him a critical once-over. He was certainly well-fed and cared for. He had loving owners somewhere, but why was he attending a wedding?

At the car, she popped out the digital memory card and stuffed it in her jacket pocket. She rewound the film in the other camera, put a sticky label on it and also put it in her jacket. As she reloaded her cameras and began to store them in the cargo bay of her car, the cat began to rub against her ankles and purr.

"Excuse me, ma'am."

She turned to face the lean man who'd been in the wedding. His chiseled features were ruggedly handsome, and his assessing gaze made her feel as if her blouse was unbuttoned. "Yes?"

"I'm afraid I can't let you leave here with those photographs," he said. His soft drawl belied the deadly sincerity in his eyes.

Michelle pushed her long red hair back. "My boss will be in touch to get all the necessary release forms."

"Your boss?"

"Iggy Adams, with *Bride Magazine.* We're

doing a feature article on brides in out-of-the-way places. Blakely State Park down here in Spanish Fort, Alabama, is pretty darn out of the way."

"I'd like the film and the digital memory cards, please."

The man was made of ice. He acted as if she'd held up a bank or something.

"That's not going to happen." She started to slam the cargo-bay door when the cat jumped in. She reached in to remove the cat, and the man put his hand on the door, blocking her.

"I'm sorry, ma'am, but you have to give me those photographs."

Whoever he was, he was trained to show no emotion. He acted as though he were asking for a piece of gum. "Those photographs are my property," she said coolly. "Now, if you want a court case, try to take them."

"No, ma'am. We don't want a court case at all. I just want those pictures. You had no right to take them."

"Look, I agree that the whole idea of photographing the wedding without notifying the bride and groom is a bit strange, but so far, every couple has been thrilled to be in *Bride Magazine*. The bride and groom will have total say over which photos are used."

"You don't understand." The man's jaw

tensed as he spoke. "Those photographs won't be used at all."

She took a breath. "Iggy won't use them if the couple refuses to sign a release. That's between them and the magazine. But Iggy paid me to come here. I've spent at least a week of time, not to mention airfare and hotels. I've got to take something back to show for the expense."

She was out of breath when she finally stopped. He was looking at her with that steely-gray gaze that said so clearly that he didn't give a damn what her story was, and he wanted what he wanted.

"Ma'am, if it were any other wedding, I'm sure the participants would be delighted to be in a fancy New York City magazine. Not this wedding, I'm afraid. Ms. Lorry asked me to get that film, and that's what I intend to do."

He reached for the camera bag, pulled it out and removed her digital camera.

Before she could blink, he had the memory card in his hand. He went for the other camera. Michelle brought the door down on his arm, not hard enough to harm him, but with enough force that he knew she meant business.

"Don't touch my equipment." She eased off the door to let him remove his arm.

"You don't understand what's at stake," he said.

She could see that he was working hard at reasoning with her. What he didn't understand was that she'd never let anyone touch her equipment. Not ever. Not for any reason. Before she could answer, she noticed the black cat had hopped to the front seat. To her amazement, the cat opened the glove box and began to rifle through the contents. "Hey!" she yelled at the cat.

The man took her moment of inattention to strip the film from her camera. He dropped the roll in his pocket and handed the camera back to her.

"Sorry, ma'am," he said.

She was furious, but she still had her photographs. Whoever this Neanderthal was, he'd only gotten blank film. The best thing she could do was beat a hasty retreat before he tried to search her.

She walked past him to the driver's door. "Shoo, kitty!" She waved her hands at the cat until he hopped out a front window. She got behind the wheel.

"Ms…." the man started.

She gunned the motor and drove out of the church parking lot like Satan was on her heels.

When she looked in the rearview mirror, he was standing there in his Confederate finery, the black cat sitting beside his polished black boots.

LUCAS WEST WATCHED THE red Alabama dust rise from the tires of the photographer's SUV, a rental from Atlanta. He memorized the tag number, but since he had the film, it was a moot issue. And it was thanks to the cat that he'd gotten the film. He looked down, but the feline had disappeared.

He stood a moment longer, pondering the strange events. Whoever the photographer was, she'd come into the wedding like a Texas tornado. He felt the corners of his mouth begin to tug into a smile. Well, maybe that was an exaggeration. She'd been quiet and professional, but the first time he'd looked at her, she'd given him a jolt. She was a looker. No doubt about that. With her lacey white shirt, tailored black slacks and stiletto boots, she'd almost stolen his breath. Until he'd seen the camera.

He sensed someone approaching and turned to face Eleanor Curry, a lovely woman who traveled with a black cat. The idea of it made him smile.

"Who was she?" Eleanor asked.

"Photographer for *Bride Magazine.*"

Eleanor whistled softly. "That's *the* magazine to be in if you're into wedding royalty."

"Lorry can't risk it. I got the film. Cockamamie idea to send a photographer to photograph a wedding without asking the bride and groom."

"It's all about that candid moment," Eleanor said as she took his arm and they walked toward the celebration in an arbor beside the church. "But you got the pictures, right? No harm done. Let's have a glass of champagne."

Lucas felt himself relax. He had the pictures; the danger had been averted. Now he wanted to enjoy this new beginning for a young woman who'd proven to be courageous and strong.

"It's wonderful to see Lorry like this," Eleanor said. "I was afraid she'd never be happy again."

"She did a very brave thing for me." Lucas took two glasses from a passing waiter and handed one to Eleanor. "I promised I'd see her into a new life. A happy life. I think this is the first step. Lorry and Charles have the whole future ahead of them."

"They're so in love." Eleanor pointed her champagne glass toward a black shadow slipping along the chairs at the buffet table. "And I'd better get Familiar. He loves wedding food, but we have to catch a flight out this evening. It's back to D.C. for a few weeks, then on to my seminar in New York. Peter will join me there when he finishes lecturing in Chicago."

"Peter's lucky to have you, Eleanor. And your cat. I know you believe he's some kind of detective, but my imagination won't stretch that far."

"Oh, Familiar will stretch it." Eleanor linked her arm through his. "Familiar has a way of letting you know exactly how smart he is. Now walk me over to kiss the bride and groom good luck. Then I'm going to retrieve my cat and head for the airport."

Chapter Two

Michelle walked through her studio, counting the photographs that would be shipped to Marco's Gallery in SoHo. Her show, a collection of black-and-white pictures that ranged from landscapes to studies of the human body, had been selected with care. Since returning home from the gig for *Bride Magazine,* she'd spent the entire three weeks working on this show.

The men would be there within the hour to carefully crate the large canvasses and then transport them to Marco's Gallery. This was a big moment, and Michelle savored it.

She toured the studio, and she stopped before each picture marked to go. The most extraordinary photograph—a bride, her gown weighted with seed pearls, a gossamer veil shading her beauty—was untagged. Michelle studied the picture, remembering the day in detail. Beside the bride was a handsome and gallant man in a gray Confederate officer's uniform. He was leaning in to kiss his bride, and the look shared between them was one of total commitment and love.

Michelle traced the scar that was barely visible on the bride's neck. She'd noticed it when she printed the picture, but she had no explanation for it. It looked as if someone had meant to cut the woman's throat, but surely that wasn't possible.

Michelle sighed. It was the finest picture she'd ever taken, but she didn't have a signed release form. No matter how good, the picture would never be shown publicly. After she'd told Iggy about the man at the wedding trying to take her film, the editor had flatly refused to even consider using the Confederate wedding photographs. Michelle had printed this one, just for herself.

She put the last tag on a picture of two horses running in a pasture in a heavy mist. They were phantom creatures, coming out of the fog, nostrils flaring. She could almost hear the hoofbeats ring on the earth.

By tomorrow morning, the art critics would have reviewed her work. They were often unkind to magazine photographers who set up shop as artists. Only time would tell how they treated her.

Her cell phone rang, and she answered it with a smile. "Sure thing, Kevin. I'll meet you in fifteen minutes. The guys are—" The sound of a knock interrupted her. "They're here now, I think. Give me a few minutes to get them started, and I'll meet up with you for that celebratory drink."

Hanging up, she opened the door. Two men from Marco's Gallery stood in the hallway, packing crates stacked neatly beside them. She showed them the numbered canvases.

"We'll take care of it, Ms. Sieck," one said. "Marco told us to use extra caution."

"Marco is a good friend. Lock the door when you leave, and be sure and tell your boss I'll be at the gallery by six-thirty this evening."

Time for a Bloody Mary with Kevin, then a facial and massage. She'd scheduled her day to be as stress-free as possible. Tonight she'd be on public display.

Clutching her handbag, she hurried to the curb to flag a taxi. This was the day she'd been waiting for. Ten years of hard work—and twenty years of dreaming. It was all out of her hands now.

LUCAS ENTERED THE AUSTIN office complex of the U.S. Marshals Service, his boots tapping on the polished tile floor. How many mornings had he come into this same office ready for a day's work? Not until Lorry Kennedy had he ever thought about quitting. Now the time was on him. He'd tendered his resignation and had only to turn in his badge and gun.

In twenty minutes, he'd no longer be a federal marshal.

As he walked down the corridor to the office, he thought about the ranch he'd bought in the Hill Country. His new life would involve cattle and horses and hard physical work. It was the remedy he'd chosen to help him deal with the death of his brother, and he was relieved to see that his fellow officers had honored his decision to quit. No one had made any effort to dissuade him.

When the official part was over, he accepted the handshakes of his fellow officers, a few jokes and back slaps, and then it was done.

As he left the building, he saw Frank Holcomb, his former partner. Frank had chosen not to be around when Lucas said his goodbyes to the rest of the guys.

"Is it official?" Frank asked.

"I'm an ordinary citizen." Lucas had to admit he felt naked without his gun and badge. "It's going to take some getting used to, but this is the way I had to play it."

"I know." Frank fell into step beside him. Once at the pickup, they stood awkwardly.

"You'll come out to the ranch. Soon. Right?" Lucas asked.

"You bet." Frank extended his hand. "I'll miss you, Lucas."

"Not too much." The moment was tougher than Lucas had expected. "Be careful, Frank."

"Will you be there for Antonio's appeal?"

Lucas felt the knot of anger that had precipitated his need to quit a job he loved. "I'll be there. Wouldn't miss it for the world."

"You take care till then."

They stood in the Texas sunshine as traffic passed beside them.

"You, too." Lucas got in the truck and pulled out into the street. It was hard to close the door on this life. Really hard. But the murder of his brother by Antonio Maxim and the near death of the only witness to that murder—Lorry Kennedy, aka Betty Sewell—had pushed Lucas too close to taking the law into his own hands.

He had to leave Antonio Maxim to the legal system while he focused on the future. Or else he'd be swallowed whole by the past.

He aimed the truck north. He had fence to ride. With enough time and enough miles on a horse, maybe he could find peace.

THERE IS NOTHING LIKE *a cool summer night in Manhattan. The city is alive all around me.*

While I love D.C. and the nearness of my most beloved Clotilde, I do enjoy a bit of Big Apple hustle.

Eleanor is preparing her speech for the linguistics conference in the morning, and I took the opportunity to sneak out and head to Marco's Gallery.

I want a peek at that long-legged siren who had Lucas so "het up" at Lorry's wedding. He was worked up good, and while 90 percent of it may have been about the photographs, the other 10 percent was that strange chemistry that sometimes happens between a man and a woman. Or a handsome black cat and his feline love.

New York is the easiest city in the nation to get around. A solitary black cat taking a relaxing ride on the subway doesn't even raise an eyebrow. I can ride beneath the city to any destination. Although, while I love New York, I have to say, if I were picking a destination spot, it would be Egypt. Now that was a trip to remember. The Egyptians understand that cats are gods, and well they should.

Here's my exit, and it's up the stairs and into the streets of SoHo. I'm so glad I snooped into Miss Shutterbug's glove box and found her schedule for the photography exhibit. I can't wait to see what her pictures look like.

I'm a little early, but the crowds are beginning to gather. Ah, the young, beautiful and sophisticated people of the city are in attendance. There's the star of the moment getting out of a limo. Wow! Be still my heart. She is a knockout in that little black dress with the crisscross straps. She is gorgeous, no doubt about it. Now let's see about talent and brains.

A few people are giving me stares, but most people don't even notice me. In a city of a thousand stories, no one is interested in one lone black cat. I'm almost invisible, which is why I'm such a successful private detective. Tonight, though, I'm off the clock. This is strictly for my pleasure.

Yeah, baby. And this exhibit is fine! The photographs are incredible. Miss Shutterbug has talent, in spades. As to the brains, perhaps that isn't important. She has enough talent to cover any lack of common sense.

The crowd agrees with me. People are captivated by her images. The one of the horses makes me want to live on a farm, as long as I don't have to ride. And that looks like the Hudson River—more of a painting than a photograph. Miss Shutterbug is amazing.

And back here is a bride and—

I'm not believing this. That's Lorry and Charles. This is not good. In fact, this is very bad. I'd better get back to the hotel and let Eleanor know about this. Something has to be done.

INHALING DEEPLY, MICHELLE reminded herself to smile and relax. Everything was going better than she'd dared to hope. A large crowd had gathered even prior to the official opening time, and she'd felt like royalty stepping out of the limo into the flash of several cameras. Marco, the gallery owner, had come through with some press coverage.

The news cameras were being set up, and while she didn't relish the idea of being filmed, if she wanted to sell her work as an artist, publicity was the name of the game. So far so good.

She allowed herself to be swept into the gallery with a cluster of socialites who'd come with checkbooks in hand. She wanted to pinch herself to make sure she wasn't hallucinating.

Photojournalism was as much a part of her as her skin, and she'd never give it up, but to be accepted as a fine artist who worked with a camera instead of paints and brushes was her dream. One she'd been afraid to reach for until Marco had encouraged her.

She walked over to the tall, distinguished gallery owner and linked her arm through his. "You are a magician!"

He kissed her cheek, beaming like her father should have, had he been able to accept her for who she, was instead of always faulting her for who she wasn't. "I merely hung these wonderful prints, Michelle. Nothing more."

"Right, fairy godmother. Where's my pumpkin coach and the white mice you turned into horses?"

His laughter echoed through the gallery. Cameras clicked and flashguns popped. "Thank you, Marco," she said as she stood on tiptoe to kiss his cheek.

"Tend to your public, Michelle." He frowned. "Did that cat come with you?"

Michelle looked in the direction he'd indicated. A beautiful black cat sat on an antique table, staring at her. It almost seemed as if the cat had singled her out. The idea was preposterous.

"No, he didn't come with me."

"If he's a stray, I think I'll keep him. He lends a certain air of sophistication to the gallery, don't you agree?"

"Indeed." Michelle strolled over and stroked the cat's back. He purred and rubbed against her. There was something very…familiar about him. "Behave, and you may have yourself a good home," she whispered to him before she went to the rear of the gallery to check on the pictures there.

She picked up a glass of champagne from a waiter and moved through the gallery, listening to the flattering comments of the guests. As she turned a corner, she saw the photograph of the Confederate wedding. She was so shocked, she stopped, forcing the traffic behind her to halt or collide with her. For seconds, she merely stared at the picture, wanting to believe that it wasn't really there.

"Darling, that's incredible. I expect that young couple to step out of the canvas and finish the kiss," a middle-aged woman said to her. "I'd like to buy it."

Michelle swallowed. She glanced around, wondering what to do. "I'm sorry, but it isn't for sale."

"I'm willing to pay a handsome price. There's something magical about that picture."

"It isn't for sale." She spoke more firmly than she'd intended. The woman huffed and walked away.

Michelle had to do something, but she didn't know what. First of all, she had to get the picture down. She had no release form signed, which meant she had no permission to exhibit the photo. She could be sued.

She slipped through several people staring at the picture and began to lift it from the hooks.

"Michelle, what are you doing?" Marco was at her side.

"It has to come down." She spoke through clenched teeth as she wrestled with the wire and hook that held it.

"It's the best of the show." Marco grasped her elbow. "What's wrong?"

"This wasn't meant to be hung," she said. Behind Marco she saw both television cameras whirring. The news crews had sensed a moment of drama and were capturing everything on film.

Holding up a hand over each lens, she tried to block them. "Stop filming," she said.

When they ignored her, she felt her temper ignite. "Stop that now. This picture isn't meant to be shown."

The crowd, which had been boisterous with laughter only moments before, grew quiet and gathered round her.

"Michelle, darling, come with me to the office," Marco said. He tried to hold her elbow, but she pulled free from him.

"Get that picture down," she said. "Please. I don't have permission—"

Marco smiled at his guests. "I've made a mistake by hanging this photograph," he said smoothly. "Could we all step to the front of the gallery while I have it replaced with the proper picture?"

As he beckoned the people to follow him,

Michelle went back to the picture. She wanted to pull it from the wall, but she knew she'd already shown far too much emotion.

She felt something brush against her legs, and she looked down at the cat. He put one gentle paw on her knee and then gave a soft meow.

As crazy as it sounded, she felt as if he sympathized with her situation.

Two workers appeared at her side and gently removed the photograph. Within moments, they reappeared with a still life to replace it.

Michelle inhaled, trying hard to calm herself. It was over now. That the photo had been hung in the show was grounds for a lawsuit, but she'd moved to correct her error instantly. The news crews would likely never use the footage they'd shot. In a city like New York, there were far bigger stories to cover than a photo exhibit.

The damage was minimal. And now she had to get back up front with Marco. He'd gotten everyone laughing at one of his jokes. She needed to prove that she wasn't some kind of psycho witch. She lifted her shoulders and walked toward the crowd.

Chapter Three

As good as room service is in this hotel, I have to say the delicacies at the photo exhibit were better. It was with great reluctance that I left that platter of roast beef crusted with fresh garlic. That gallery owner, Marco, is a man with a discriminating palate. His offer to take me in has a lot of merit. I wonder if I could merely visit. Naturally, I'd never abandon Eleanor and Peter. They adore me, and they need me. But a SoHo party address would be a nice coup.

But enough about my limitless possibilities. It's time for the news, and I want to be sure that Eleanor is watching. Those cameras were certainly whirring, capturing Michelle Sieck's moment of high drama as she tried to yank her photograph off the wall.

If this is used in a newscast, Eleanor needs to know—because Lorry could be in danger.

Ah, here's the local segment of WKPT and the gala crowd at the photo exhibit. They're using the gallery event as the lead local story. I have a feeling this is going to be bad.

Eleanor doesn't realize the significance yet, but she will. Let me put my claws in her shin just a little to keep her attention from wandering.

Okay, we're at the part where Michelle creates a commotion. There're the photographs. And Michelle makes it all worse by putting her hand over the lens for a moment. She should never have done that. That really torques a cameraman off, and she should know that better than anyone else.

Oh, cupid in a diaper, they're showing the photograph of Lorry. It is so stunning that people are compelled to study it. The scar on Lorry's neck is visible. Someone who knew what she looked like could easily recognize her, even through the gauze of the veil.

This is bad. Really, really bad. Eleanor is dialing her cell phone. I can tell from the tension in her body that she's distressed.

"Hello, Lucas. This is Eleanor Curry. I'm afraid we have an emergency situation. I just saw a photograph of Lorry Kennedy on a New York news station. They were covering a gallery opening, and Lorry's picture was part of a brouhaha where that photographer woman *tried to keep them from filming it. It won't be hard for the Maxims to retrace that photographer's steps. I'm afraid Lorry's cover has been blown."*

THE CELL PHONE WAS CHILLY against Lucas's ear. Camped on one of the isolated sites on his ranch, he'd hoped the peace of the land and the beauty of the stars would finally lull him to sleep. Deep down, though, he'd had a sense that trouble would come a-calling.

His sixth sense had often saved him from a mouthful of knuckles—or worse, a bullet. He'd been teased by the other marshals, who accused him of consulting psychics and having a hotline to the Jamaican television personality who'd made great claims about her abilities to predict the future.

Lucas, like most of his fellow law enforcement officials, was skeptical about psychic abilities, but he had absolute faith in his gut.

When the cell phone rang, Tazer, his little blue heeler, began to growl. The phone and the dog's reaction to it made the hair on the back of Lucas's neck prickle.

This was not good news.

When he realized it was Eleanor, he was relieved and surprised. Until he heard her first statement.

"When was this?" he asked. He began to kick dirt over his campfire.

"Earlier this evening."

"Damn." He wasn't a man who cursed, but this was terrible. He'd been a fool. The red-headed photographer at Lorry's wedding had played him like a fine fiddle. He'd taken her film, and she hadn't even threatened a lawsuit. And now he knew why. The film and memory card he'd taken and destroyed had, in all probability, been blank.

"I've got to find Lorry," he said. She and Charles had gone on a honeymoon, and then they were moving, beginning that new life she'd risked everything to have. Though he felt as if Lorry were the little sister he'd never had, he'd let her go without any questions, knowing he'd see her at Antonio's final appeal. The fewer people who knew where she was, the less the danger of the Maxims ever finding her.

"You find that photographer," Eleanor said. "Find her, get the film or whatever, and put an end to this. If she's showing that picture anywhere else, we have to stop it."

"I'll book a flight to New York and call *Bride Magazine* in the morning. I'll make her editor tell me how to get in touch with her."

"No need. Michelle Sieck's work is in Marco's Gallery in SoHo."

"How did you happen to watch that particular newscast?" Lucas asked. It was lucky Eleanor had seen it, but what were the odds?

"Familiar made sure I saw it. I told you, he's a detective. And a darn good one."

Lucas didn't have time to argue with Eleanor about a cat's ability to sleuth out pertinent information. He found it odd, though, that a woman of such high intelligence could believe such a load of poppycock.

MICHELLE BURIED HER FACE in her hands as the news story continued to spill across the screen. The whole business with the Confederate picture had been a comedy of errors. And the bottom line was, she should never have printed it.

Surely, though, nothing truly awful could happen because of the mistake at the gallery. If only the media hadn't covered the event. If only she hadn't put her hand up to block the cameras. She knew better, but she'd acted on impulse. The wrong impulse. She stepped outside for a breath of fresh air.

Around her the celebration of her highly successful exhibit continued unabated. Kevin—her oldest friend in the city—and Marco were proposing toasts. A dozen friends were at the bar to show their support. This should have been a moment of elation. Instead, she was worried sick.

"Michelle, what are you doing here by yourself?"

Kevin Long was a fashion photographer who worked for the biggest names in the industry. His blond hair, a halo of curls, made him look angelic.

"Too much emotion." She twirled the stem of her wineglass. "I needed a moment to gather my wits. It's been hectic."

"Hectic and successful. You should be dancing on the tables, but instead, you're acting like you've just lost your best friend." He put his arm around her and gave her a hug. "I'm sorry your parents didn't show."

She'd been so absorbed in the picture fiasco that she'd failed to even acknowledge the hurt generated by her parents. They'd wanted her to become a doctor. They felt photography was a hobby, not a career. In their generally disapproving way, they'd simply refused to acknowledge any success she had in her chosen field. Friends like Kevin and Marco were her support system.

"I didn't expect them to come." She forced a wry smile. "It's okay. They love me. They just don't understand me."

"You'd think they would be proud."

"Maybe they are, in their own way. They're just more stubborn than proud. But your folks came, and they're like my second parents. That was plenty good enough for me."

"Mom and Dad view you like a daughter, Michelle. You know that. In fact, if it came to a choice between the two of us…they'd pick you."

Her laughter wasn't forced. Kevin was an outrageous liar, and he always made her feel better. "Let's join the party." Marco was still proposing toasts, and if she didn't get in there and break it up, no one would be able to stand long enough to flag a taxi home.

As she turned to go back inside, she noticed a long black car parked at the curb, motor running. No one had gotten in or out of it. It was almost as if someone was in the car waiting…for what? A prickle of goose bumps ran up her neck. She shook her head. She'd watched way too many movies.

THE AUSTIN AIRPORT WAS quiet, and Lucas put his booted feet on his overnight bag, tipped his hat over his face and decided to catch forty winks. He'd gotten a ticket on a late-night flight to Dallas, where he'd take a midnight special to New York. He'd be at Michelle Sieck's door before the rooster sang in the morning.

As he sought sleep, he tried to steer his thoughts away from Lorry and where she might be—or who might be tracking her right this minute.

The truth was, if the Maxim family connections in New York had seen the story on the photo exhibit, Michelle could be in as much danger as Lorry.

He'd almost drifted off when he had a terrible image of Michelle in the hands of Robert Maxim, Antonio's younger brother. Word on the street was that Robert was more brutal, more sadistic than Antonio had ever thought to be.

The image was so disturbing that Lucas gave up on resting. He went to the concession stand, where a lone Latino woman was reading a magazine behind the counter. She smiled at his request and made a fresh pot of coffee for him.

When he had his large black coffee, he went back to his seat, pulled a notepad out of his pocket and began to make notes.

Antonio Maxim had been sentenced to life in prison on a charge of first-degree murder. The Maxim family ran an underground white slavery ring, luring young Texas girls to the big city with a promise of modeling and acting careers, only to hook them on drugs and turn them out on the streets.

The life expectancy for such a girl was eight years. If they weren't rescued, many of them died of diseases borne of the drugs that kept them numbed to life. More than a few ended up as suicides. Some were murdered because they were at the wrong place at the wrong time.

Lucas's brother, Harry, had been sent undercover from the Dallas Police Department up to New York to get evidence on the Maxim family. He'd done just that, but someone had blown his cover.

Harry had been standing on the corner of a busy intersection in broad daylight when a black Mercedes had pulled up in front of him. In one of the boldest killings in the city in recent years, Antonio had stepped out of the car long enough to shoot Harry point-blank in the heart and head. He'd died within seconds.

Lucas knew the fine details of the murder because of Lorry Kennedy's courage. Known at that time as Betty Sewell, she'd been in the vicinity by happenstance—a dance audition— and her thoughts had been on many things other than her physical surroundings. At the trial that resulted in Antonio's conviction for murder, Lorry testified that she'd come around the corner just in time to see Antonio step from the car, shove the gun in Harry's chest and pull the trigger. Antonio was smiling when he did it.

Survival instincts had kicked in, and Lorry had dropped her bag and run for her life. She'd escaped, but three days later, Antonio and his men had found her. Antonio had given the order to cut her throat, and his men were in the process of doing just that when Lucas had arrived. He'd killed three of Antonio's men on the spot and gotten Lorry to a hospital.

The doctors hadn't been certain Lorry would live, but she had. And she was hopping mad. She made certain that Antonio went to prison for the rest of his life.

Now the last hurdle was his appeal. If something happened to Lorry, then the case against Antonio would be extremely weak. Antonio knew that, as did his brother, Robert. And Robert would do whatever it took to get his big brother out of prison.

Whatever it took.

Killing Lorry. Killing Michelle Sieck. Whatever it took.

Lucas swallowed the rest of his coffee and stood. He could see the plane outside the window. Soon he'd board. Then he'd find that photographer. She'd endangered Lorry and herself.

The Maxims wouldn't care what Michelle knew or didn't know. If there was even the slimmest chance that she could lead them to Lorry, they'd dig it out of her by any means necessary.

Chapter Four

Michelle awoke the next morning with a pounding headache. She'd had only two glasses of champagne, so the throbbing behind her eyes must be tension-related. The events of yesterday had caught up with her in a physical way.

She rolled over and snatched a pillow to cover her head. It was just after six, a time meant for sleep.

The hard knock at her door didn't register until it came for the second time, a series of poundings that said someone meant business.

Thinking that it might be something to do with Marco and the gallery, she grabbed her old chenille robe and went to the door.

"Hold your horses. I'm coming!" She was grumpy and she didn't care. She cracked the door on the chain and felt as if she'd stepped into someone else's life. The tall man from the

Confederate wedding was standing outside her apartment. Except he was wearing jeans, cowboy boots and a Stetson—exactly as she'd imagined him.

"Michelle Sieck," he said in a voice like someone on *Law and Order.* "I'm Lucas West. Please open the door. Now."

"Why are *you* here?"

"I could tell you a pack of lies and get in the door, but I'm going to give it to you straight because a woman's life may be on the line. The woman in that wedding picture you took is a federally protected witness. You've blown her cover and endangered her life. Now your life may also be in danger. Open the door so we can begin to make this right."

Michelle slowly undid the latch. She stepped back, moving zombielike to the kitchen. "I need some coffee," she said.

"There's no time." Lucas scanned the room and walked to the windows. After he checked the street, he lowered the blinds and pulled the curtains shut.

"I'm dying from a headache. I need caffeine."

"We'll get some at the airport."

She tried to focus on what he was saying, but things were moving too fast. "The airport?"

He wheeled on her then, the anger she'd seen

clearly in his gray eyes and terse expression no longer under control. "Lorry Kennedy's life could be at stake. Likely Charles's, too. Because of you. Because you did exactly what you wanted to do with a photograph that never should have been taken."

Michelle stumbled backward from the onslaught of his harsh words. Once she regained her balance, though, she stepped into his face.

"I didn't intend to show that photograph. The movers picked it up by mistake. As soon as I saw it, I had it removed."

"And you think that makes it okay?" Lucas glared at her.

She lifted her chin and looked into his flinty eyes. "It doesn't make it okay, but it doesn't make me a worthless liar, either. It was an accident."

"So if Robert Maxim finds Lorry and kills her, we can just mark it down as an accidental death."

Her head was throbbing so hard, she thought she might throw up. Preferably on his boots. She *hated* to have her nose rubbed in a mistake. Her parents were masters at this behavior and had shoved every tiny misstep back in her face. Until she'd found the grit to move to New York and follow her dream.

"That's not what I meant," she said through

clenched teeth. "All I'm saying is that this didn't happen because I didn't care." She held up her hands. Why was she trying to explain this to a cowboy?

"Pack a bag. I've got to get you out of here. If I can find you, so can the Maxims."

"I'm not going anywhere, and you aren't going to panic me into doing something insane, like get on a plane with a man I don't know at all and who may himself be a psycho killer."

Lucas laughed, but it wasn't from amusement. "That scar on Lorry's neck?"

He watched her like a hawk, waiting for the moment to pounce. She wanted to squirm, but she wouldn't allow herself. "I saw the scar."

"Antonio Maxim ordered his men to cut her throat and throw her in the river so she couldn't testify against him. He'll do worse to you, because he'll want information."

His words were having an effect, though she would die before she let him see it. "And what did this Antonio Maxim do that was so awful?"

Lucas glanced down, but only for a split second. When he locked eyes with Michelle again, he looked madder than ever. "He killed my brother, an undercover cop, and he's responsible for hundreds of young girls ending up as prostitutes and drug addicts. Is that bad enough for you?"

She found a chair with her hand and slowly lowered her body into it. Murder, forced prostitution, drugs. She wasn't an innocent. She knew the city had a million layers, and at the bottom there was a lot of pain and suffering.

Never had she expected to find it on her doorstep, though.

"Is Lorry okay?"

"My friend has been trying to find her since that newscast aired last night. As of this morning, both she and Charles have vanished."

Michelle felt as if someone had kicked her in the gut. "Vanished as in left by their own choice, or vanished as in someone took them?"

"I won't be able to tell until I look. That's why you're packing a bag and we're going to Mobile, Alabama. As much as I'd like to put you in a safe house, I can't. I'm Lorry's best chance at survival, and you're going with me."

Michelle was about to protest when she heard the strangest sound.

"What's that?" She rose slowly. It sounded as if someone was scratching wood.

She started toward the door, but Lucas pulled her back and stepped in front of her. He moved with grace and authority.

His hand went to his side, and she knew instinctively that he was reaching for a weapon. Whatever he'd done in his past, he was used to carrying a firearm. But his hand came back empty. For once, she would have been glad to see some kind of gun in someone's hand.

The scratching came again.

When Lucas looked out the peephole of her door, he muttered under his breath.

"Who is it?" she asked.

"There's no one there."

Yet the scratching came once more.

Lucas opened the door slowly. They both looked down at the black cat, which stared back up at them.

"Is that the cat from the wedding and from the gallery?" Michelle asked. Along with her pounding head, she was now suffering from hallucinations.

"I'll be…a five-toed Texas longhorn." Lucas stepped back, and the cat entered the room with an air of royalty.

"How does he get around town?" Michelle asked.

"Danged if I know," Lucas answered. "But he does. Eleanor swears he's a private investigator. He gets calls from all around the world."

Pressing her hands to her temples, Michelle headed to the small kitchen. She put on the pot for coffee. The man ordering her around her own apartment could just wait until she got a jolt of caffeine in her system. She couldn't deal with murderers, dead brothers, witness protection and cats who solved mysteries without some coffee. Something much stronger might even be better.

INSTEAD OF ARGUING, LUCAS yielded on the coffee. Time was short, but it would do no good to bully Michelle. He'd seen her distress, and he knew it was real. She'd never intended for any of the events that had taken place to occur. He sure knew what that felt like.

While Michelle brewed the coffee, he called Eleanor and told her Familiar had shown up.

"I told you," Eleanor said. "Let him help you, Lucas. He has a gift."

"I'm finding this a bit hard to swallow."

She laughed. "It's tough on the U.S. marshal ego to rely on a cat, but he will help, if you let him. He's fond of Lorry, and he's got a thing for that photographer. Familiar has excellent taste in women. He picked me out to be his owner."

Lucas couldn't help but smile. It was an intrguing concept—that the cat had an interest in Michelle. But he had shown up at the gallery and now at her apartment. No. It was too crazy to concede.

"When we leave, I'll call you, and you can come and pick him up."

"Okay."

He hung up and went to the kitchen, where he laid out the travel plans for Michelle. Her color was better as she sipped the strong black coffee. His cup remained untouched. He was already jittery. Too much adrenaline and too little sleep.

"We'll take the eleven o'clock flight south. I've already booked us seats."

"I'm not going." Michelle's hazel eyes dared him to contradict her.

He was happy to oblige. "You are. I've already told you that it's dangerous to stay here. They know you saw Lorry. They're going to be looking for you, and when they catch you, it won't do any good to say you don't know her. You photographed her wedding. They *will* hurt you."

"I'm not going."

His temper jumped so high, he felt the pulse in his jaw. Why was Michelle being so ornery when he was trying to save her from being hurt?

"You're going, and you're going to behave." He could see that his authoritative manner was only antagonizing her more.

"I'm going to shower and dress." She downed the last of the coffee and stood.

"Now that's a sensible way to act."

She didn't comment as she left the room and went to what he presumed was her bathroom, to get ready. He drummed his fingers on the table and watched the black cat, who was snooping around the apartment.

A cat detective. Even in Texas, where the tales were tall, he'd never heard of such a thing.

The cat sashayed out of the kitchen, and he was left alone with his thoughts. Lorry would be careful. She knew what was at stake, and she'd take precautions. Once he found her place, he'd search it and figure out where she might have gone. But he had to get there first, before Robert Maxim sent some of his goons.

He paced the kitchen, and as he moved toward the narrow hallway, he heard the shower running. He checked his watch. Ten minutes. How long did it take a woman to shower?

Moving back to the table, he sat and drummed his fingers more. Patience was not one of his virtues, and the years of working as a law officer hadn't helped any. That was one of the things he loved about the job. Action and more action.

Harry had loved his work, too. He thought about his brother, how he'd been so excited about going to New York undercover. Harry had been caught up in the case of a young

Austin girl who'd disappeared. Her trail had led straight to New York and Antonio Maxim.

The NYPD had found her body in a Dumpster outside a fleabag hotel. She'd been loaded with drugs and then stabbed. It had deeply disturbed Harry, and his investigation of Antonio Maxim had become personal. Very personal.

A loud cry came from the living room. It sounded like a cat in distress. He jumped to his feet just as the door slammed.

Dang it all to hell and back! He was across the living room and into the hall just in time to see Michelle disappear down the stairs. The crazy woman was running away from him. The black cat was right on her heels.

He was a flight of stairs behind her, and once she got to the street, she might disappear into the crowds of pedestrians that streamed down the city sidewalks.

"Michelle!" He called her name, but she didn't slow. "Michelle! Don't do this!"

He was on the sidewalk when he saw her at the bus stop, moving fast. To his utter amazement, the black cat darted between her feet.

In another moment, she was sprawling on the sidewalk, cursing the cat like a whorehouse hussy. Lucas jogged to her side.

He offered her a hand and pulled her to her feet. "That's some impressive language."

She gave him a look that would curdle goat milk. "That cat tripped me on purpose."

"So it would seem." Lucas bent down to stroke Familiar's back. The cat purred and rubbed against his legs. "Glad to see at least *he* has good sense. I guess I owe Eleanor an apology."

"He could have broken my neck."

"Which would be a lot less painful than what the Maxims will do to you if they catch you." Lucas surveyed the area. Except for a black car with heavily tinted windows parked halfway down the block, motor running, nothing looked suspicious. The car was expensive and could easily be a hired car or ride for a corporate type. Then again, Antonio Maxim didn't hire thugs who looked like thugs. His men maintained the appearance of white-collar professionals. The car made him nervous. "Let's go," he said to Michelle.

She dusted her hands on her jeans and started back toward the apartment. Lucas walked beside her, the cat right in step with them both.

"We're taking the cat to Mobile," he said.

When he didn't get an argument from Michelle, he hid the grin that touched his mouth and made his eyes crinkle. It was a small victory, but a victory nonetheless.

Now all they had to do was get to the airport and board their flight—without being followed.

Chapter Five

By the time the plane touched down in Mobile, Michelle had gone from seething to worried. Her actions, though innocent, had created a landslide of possible tragedy. No matter how she thought it through, she'd put a woman at risk. Not to mention herself, provided Lucas wasn't exaggerating.

He'd been a gentleman for the entire trip, making sure she had food and coffee and something to read, but she could tell he viewed her as the cause of trouble. The accusation was there in his intense gray gaze.

The cat, on the other hand, had curled up in her lap and gone to sleep, waking only to charm the flight attendant out of some heavy whipping cream. He was certainly a special creature.

As they walked through the small Mobile airport, she glanced at Lucas. He was a handsome man, even when he was displeased—which seemed to be most of the time. And he was as edgy as a cat on a fence. He kept looking behind him, and then left and right, as if he expected the bad guys to jump out from behind a potted shrub. Or that she was going to make a break for freedom. She bit her lip at the memory of her failed escape.

Lucas had good reason to be annoyed with her, but she wasn't going to apologize again. Apologies wouldn't change a blasted thing, and she'd done it once and meant it. If he couldn't accept it, that was his issue, not hers.

Lucas rented a car, and they drove through the old downtown of the port city that had served under seven flags of occupation. In the older parts of town, where developers hadn't run rampant, oak trees canopied the street.

The antebellum homes, set back from the road, on lawns filled with the floral frills of a subtropical climate, spoke to Michelle of another time, when chivalry and honor were supposed to be important. How in the world had she ended up in such a mess as this? She'd only wanted to do her job, to take photographs.

They entered a tunnel that went beneath the Mobile River, and when they reemerged, she looked out the window on glittering Mobile Bay, which she remembered from her previous trip. Lucas ignored the beauty of the scene, focusing entirely on his driving and on watching the rearview mirror. Even the cat kept looking behind them. She glanced back, wondering if she'd be able to detect a tail if there was one behind them. The idea made her distinctly uncomfortable, so she focused on the road ahead of them.

They were close now. She could only hope that they'd find Lorry and Charles safely at home, honeymooning and not answering the phone. Once Lucas had Lorry safely in his care, maybe he'd let her return to New York and her life.

"What happens when we find her?" Michelle asked.

"I'll get her back to Austin. The marshals will help her get a new identity." He gave Michelle a hard look. "And you, too."

"Me, too, what?" Michelle asked. The bottom had dropped out of her stomach.

"A new identity. The Maxim family won't give up, Michelle. You've stepped into this now, and if you'll pardon the Texas slang, you've got it all over your boots. You're tracking it behind you, and there's no way around it."

"I will not give up my identity." The very idea of it made her want to open the car door and risk bodily harm in an attempt to escape Lucas. "Do you have any idea how hard I've worked to build a name and reputation? The years of—"

"Is it worth your life?"

"That's not a fair question."

"Do you think what happened to Lorry is fair? She stumbled on a murder. She lost her family, everything. And now she's going to have to lose it a second time, because of you. Talk to me about what's fair now."

Michelle couldn't answer. The lump in her throat was too big, too painful. Everything Lucas said was true. Had she never printed the photograph, none of this would have happened. Her moment of vanity had brought this down on the heads of everyone involved.

They crossed the bay and turned left at the intersection.

"I'm sorry," Lucas said softly. "That was cruel, and I shouldn't have said it that way."

"It's true. How else is there to say it?" She stared straight ahead, fighting to control her emotions and the rising panic.

"You didn't mean for this to happen, but it has. Now the easiest thing for all of us is to deal with it. To figure out the safest thing for you and Lorry and make sure that happens."

"My name is everything. If I have to change

it, I won't have a career or a way to make a living."

Lucas sighed. "People adapt, Michelle. A different life is better than being tortured to death. That's what will happen if the Maxims get their hands on you."

"What if we can't find Lorry?" As soon as the question was out of her mouth, the black cat sat up and put a paw on her lips.

"Listen to the cat," Lucas said. "Don't go there. Don't even think that."

"Shouldn't you call in the feds?" she asked.

She knew it was the wrong question by the way his hands clenched the steering wheel. The truth was, it seemed that no question she asked was the right one. He'd made her feel like crap, and now he was acting like she was a nitwit.

"What? Did I say something wrong? Isn't it normal to call in the FBI when a person is presumed to have been kidnapped and possibly tortured because she's a witness in a murder case?"

"You can't let it go, can you?" Lucas responded, his hands tightening on the wheel.

"No, I can't. You're telling me I have to reinvent myself, but you won't answer a single question."

"Here's your answer then. Someone blew

my brother's cover. I can't prove anything, but I don't trust the FBI, the marshals or anyone else. Lorry is my responsibility, and like it or not, so are you. Lorry is in this because she wanted to help me achieve justice for my brother's murder. She could have run away or 'forgotten' what she saw." But she stood her ground and told the truth. Now, because of your photo, she could be killed. So I'll find Lorry, and I'll protect her. Once Antonio's appeal is over, maybe we can put this behind us. Until then, I can't risk putting my trust in anyone. Not the feds, not the marshals, not even my partner, who was like a brother to me."

She remembered the way his hand had gone for a gun. "You're a cop, too, aren't you?"

"Not anymore."

She could tell he didn't want to talk about it, but so what? She didn't want to be in the car with him. "What kind of cop?"

"A federal one. Not FBI."

"So your brother worked for the Dallas police and you were with the U.S. marshals?"

He gave her a look that told her to shut up and back off.

"Is your dad in law enforcement?"

His sigh was long and loud. "My past is my business, Michelle. Drop it, okay?"

"So you're the only one who can ask questions?"

"Ask questions about something else."

"Like what? The weather? It isn't as if we share a whole bunch of interests. What about golf? Is that a good topic?" She was deviling him now, and it was satisfying.

She felt the cat's sharp claws dig into her thigh. "Ouch!"

Lucas laughed, and she saw what he might look like if he didn't carry the weight of the world on his shoulders. He was a striking man.

"Are you married?" she asked.

"Man, you just go from bad to worse, don't you?"

"Divorced, eh?" She felt a moment of strange kinship. "Must have been bad, too, from the way you're acting."

He drove in silence, and she looked out the window. They'd circled around and cut through the woods, so that they were cresting a high bluff that gave frequent glimpses of the bay flashing by. She was struck by a memory, and she spoke before she thought. "You know, when I was a kid, I came to Alabama to camp. A photography camp. That was the best summer of my life."

She felt his gaze on her, but she kept her eyes focused out the window. The water was beautiful in the afternoon light. How was it possible that only a few weeks earlier, she'd crossed the same body of water on her way to photograph a wedding? Her world had been in order. She'd been dreaming of her gallery opening, something that she'd walked away from without even a phone call to Marco. Lucas hadn't allowed her to contact anyone.

Her cell phone was in her purse, and she could call the gallery owner as soon as she got a moment alone, but Lucas had warned her that anyone she drew into her web of trouble could be hurt.

She wouldn't put Marco or Kevin at risk. They would worry for her, but worry was better than being tortured or killed. And for whatever strange reason, she believed Lucas. He wasn't the kind of man who exaggerated the danger that now surrounded her and Lorry.

"I know you didn't mean for this to happen," Lucas said.

She wanted to pretend to clean her ears, as if she hadn't heard properly. Sarcasm had always been her best defense. Instead, she asked, "What if Lorry is hurt?"

"Think positive, but be on the alert for negative."

"Is that the lawman's code?" Her emotions shifted yet again, and she found tears welling in her eyes. She didn't like to cry in front of people. Had never liked it. She'd been taught it was a weakness, and her parents detested weakness in any form.

"It's my code. Look, I'm sorry I snapped at you and accused you of things."

"It was the truth."

Familiar stretched and licked her chin, giving her comfort she hadn't realized she craved. He used his head to butt her cheek, and she felt her spirits lift a little.

"Truth is a strange thing, Michelle. You could never have known why I didn't want Lorry's picture taken. I couldn't tell you. After I saw the photograph, I understood why you wanted a print for yourself."

"It was meant only for me. It may be the best work I've ever done, but I would never deliberately have shown it without permission."

He took a single-track lane deep into the beautiful woods.

"Let's make a deal," Lucas said. "We put the past behind us. We forget how all this began and simply do our best to bring it to the right conclusion."

She wanted to nod, but something held her back. Guilt? Remorse? Stubbornness? She wasn't certain. "I'm sorry you got dragged into this. You've had enough loss."

"This was part of my job. I'm not a lawman anymore, so this time I'm not bound by the conduct that governs law officers."

His voice was so cold and deadly that a chill slid over her. "What does that mean?"

"It means that as an officer of the law, I was sworn to bring Antonio in alive. Or at least to try to."

"And now?"

"If Robert or any of his goons have harmed Lorry, I'll do whatever I have to do."

She swallowed. A question stuck in her throat. Sometimes it was best not to know. As they turned down a tree-shaded lane toward a lovely cottage, she realized that she'd just learned her first valuable lesson from Lucas.

EVER SINCE LUCAS GOT LORRY and Charles's address from Eleanor, he's been focused on getting to Spanish Fort. I didn't see anything suspicious in the Mobile airport, but I had the sense that we were being followed at Kennedy. There were men outside Michelle's apartment this morning. Lucas saw them. He did his best to give them the slip, getting the cab driver to head toward Brooklyn and then veer off to the airport. I'm not certain he was successful, though. This Maxim organization has a long reach....

Michelle is wallowing in guilt. Both of them have forgotten that a cat needs sustenance. The cream on the plane was a nice surprise, but let's just say I'm not the type of cat who likes a liquid diet. The bipeds don't understand that I need small, frequent meals. It's part of my diet plan to maintain my svelte figure.

So here's Lorry's cottage. Cute as a button, and just exactly what I would have imagined. Big screened porch to watch the sunset over the bay, shady lawn with that lush green grass that folks around here call Centipede. It's heavenly.

And a kitchen stocked with food. Let's see. Once I find something edible, my brain will work better. Hmm, a small tin of sardines. Well, it isn't up to my normal standards, but if I can get Miss Shutterbug's attention, she can open it for me.

Ah, she's not as self-absorbed as she acts. She has it open and has dumped it in a saucer for me. A tasty little snack to tide me over until mealtime. Fish oil is vital to the health of my coat, after all.

Now let's see. Lucas is searching the living room. And Michelle has the bedroom, though she doesn't even have a grasp of what she might be looking for. I'll take the bathroom. Always a few good clues there.

The medicine cabinet is empty. Now that's a

big clue. Most people take only what they need for a trip. This bathroom has been stripped down. And I hear Michelle.

"LUCAS, SOME OF THE DRAWERS in here are empty. It looks like all of Lorry's personal items are all gone."

UH-OH. A PERSON doesn't pack everything for a honeymoon. Not even a long one. This doesn't look good.

Chapter Six

Leaving Michelle searching inside, Lucas went over the garage. Time was slipping away. He was already far behind. He couldn't say why, but he had the sense that the Maxims had been to the cottage first. They'd been—and gone. With Lorry and Charles? That was the question.

While he was out of Michelle's sight, he pulled out his cell phone and dialed *Bride Magazine.* He used Michelle's name to get to Iggy Adams, and when he had the editor on the phone, he realized that his worst suspicions were in order.

"Yes, I did get a call early this morning regarding a photograph Michelle took," Iggy said in answer to his question.

"What did you tell them?"

"I didn't have a lot to tell," she said. "It was someone asking about the bridal photo that caused such a stir on the news. I told them she'd taken the picture in Baldwin County, Alabama."

Lucas wanted to hit the wall with his fist. He should have called the magazine and warned them not to discuss Michelle.

"Is something wrong?" Iggy asked.

"Michelle is in danger." He didn't know how tough to play it. "She's okay now, but that photograph has put her in harm's way. Please don't discuss it with anyone else. Don't reveal anything about Michelle to anyone."

"How do I know I should trust *you?*" Iggy was nobody's fool.

"You don't. But you have to, anyway. If anyone calls and asks, as far as you know, Michelle is on assignment in Africa."

"You'd better keep her safe."

"That's my goal." He hung up, still kicking himself for not calling the magazine sooner. The Maxims had undoubtedly tracked Michelle to Alabama. And his gut told him that they'd beaten him to the cottage.

While he couldn't dispute that Lorry and Charles were gone, the fact that they'd packed so many personal items made him feel better. It looked as if the two newlyweds had prepared to make a run for it, knowing there would be no coming back to this wonderful and secluded cottage.

If that assumption was true, Lorry was aware of the fact that she was in danger; it also told him she was at least one step ahead of Robert Maxim and his thugs. Now he had to figure out how to keep it that way.

He found nothing useful in the garage and moved on to the outside of the house. Tire tracks from the vehicle that had been inside the garage were clearly visible in the dirt, and he followed them to the main road, where he stopped. A second set of trademarks from a larger vehicle told another story.

The vehicle had pulled up to the edge of the property, braked enough to leave skid marks and left. It would be an educated guess that the car belonged to someone from Maxim's organization. But before or after Lorry and Charles left?

What might have happened made his gut knot.

He started back to the house and saw the black cat in the window, pawing the glass to get his attention.

What the hell? What was going on now?

He increased his speed and entered the front door. Every sense alert, he paused, taking in the quietness of the house, the cat racing toward him, the lack of sound from the kitchen.

Where was Michelle?

He wanted to call out, but he'd spent too

many years working as a cop to give his position away by yelling. Instead, he swept through the front of the house, toward the kitchen, as stealthily as the black cat at his side. He let his body move into the patterns of a skilled officer while he focused on listening.

Glass rattled in the kitchen. He picked up a heavy brass figurine as a weapon. Where was Michelle? Had someone slipped into the house, surprised her and hurt her? The idea of it made him grip the figurine harder. He'd been a fool to turn in his gun. This business with the Maxim brothers wouldn't be finished until Antonio had exhausted his last appeal and Robert was behind bars with him.

Grief at his brother's murder had pushed him to take a rash action. Now he was in a dangerous place, with no weapon.

Just as he pushed at the door, something smashed on the tile floor in the kitchen.

"Damn it!" Michelle said.

Lucas lowered his makeshift club and inhaled. "You okay?" he asked.

"Fine. I just broke a wineglass. Probably one of her wedding gifts. I wonder if I can do any more damage in this woman's life."

He eased the door open and stepped inside to find Michelle kneeling as she swept up the glass. "I'm sure it can be replaced," he said.

"I hope so." She rose slowly, not meeting his gaze.

"It's a glass. Don't make it a big issue." Her hangdog attitude worked on him far quicker than her bluster or defensiveness. He'd been pretty hard on her, and she would suffer, too. As she'd pointed out, she'd lost a life she'd worked hard to build.

She put the broken pieces of glass in the trash, her face shielded by her beautiful red hair. "Find anything?"

"Nothing that tells me where Lorry might have gone." He didn't want to mention the second set of tire prints. Michelle was on edge enough.

"What do we do now?" she asked.

"Some food, and then a hotel, I guess."

Dusk had fallen, and with the fading of the light, he was touched with a familiar sadness. He hated this time of day, when activity ended. When he was growing up on the West ranch in the Texas panhandle, the end of the day had been a time to celebrate with a filling supper and stories of history and adventure. He, his parents and his brother had been a close family, one that worked the land and struggled together. This time of day had always been filled with love.

The problem with family hour was that it required a family to make it work.

Michelle pushed her hair back from her face. "I'm beat. Lucas, can I call the gallery? Marco is going to be worried sick."

He considered it. Although he wasn't on the payroll any longer, he needed to check in with the agency. "Let me call the marshals in Texas and have them relay a message to him. The less he knows, the safer he is."

She conceded without a single argument, and he wanted to reach out and touch her forehead to see if she might be running a fever. In his limited experience with the redhead, she never gave up a point without a fight.

"You want some dinner?" he asked.

She didn't have time to answer before the cat jumped from the kitchen counter into his arms.

"Familiar is ready to eat," Michelle said, and the hint of a smile was magical. Lucas found himself wondering what other things could put a smile on her face.

"Then let's find some chow. This area is known for its seafood restaurants."

"Sounds like a plan."

THE WINE WAS DELICIOUS, cold and crisp, a surprise. Michelle hadn't expected Lucas to be a connoisseur of the grape, but he'd selected the best of the offerings. She sipped hers and thought about the brochure she'd found in the kitchen—the one she'd tucked into the waistband of her jeans just as Lucas had come unexpectedly into the kitchen.

He'd almost caught her.

The cat had tried to rat her out—pawing on the window like a demented creature to get Lucas's attention—but so far, Lucas was unaware of what she'd discovered under the refrigerator. It had probably fallen free of the magnets that held other notes to the metal frame.

The brochure wasn't much. Probably not anything. Just a pamphlet that showed white-sand beaches and gentle aqua waves. Gulf Shores, a resort community a little over an hour away from where they were.

Maybe it was where Lorry and Charles had honeymooned, but Michelle didn't think so. Most newlyweds wanted the unfamiliar, and Gulf Shores was too close to be an exotic honeymoon locale.

But it was a perfect hiding place, because it was in plain sight. And she had an address with a condo unit number written on the brochure. If her hunch was right, she'd find Lorry and Charles before the night was over.

And then she'd use herself as bait to draw the Maxim people after her while Lorry and Charles escaped.

She'd given it a lot of thought, and this whole mess was her fault. The only thing she could do to rectify it would be to lure the thugs away from Lorry and Charles and to herself. If she could get the attention of the Maxim organization and tempt them into chasing her, then Lucas would be free to keep Lorry safe. This wouldn't undo the damage she'd done by printing that picture, but it would be a step in the right direction.

She watched Lucas eat his grilled shrimp. He'd gone to a lot of trouble to find a restaurant with a private dining area so they could eat without fear of being seen. It was one of the most considerate things anyone had ever done for her. Which made her feel only that much worse.

What she planned to do wasn't exactly an ethical thing, but in the long run, it would work out for the best. He could focus on protecting Lorry, and she'd take care of herself. She'd always taken care of herself, so this wouldn't be such a big deal. She'd stay on the move, going in unexpected directions and not contacting anyone.

The thought that she'd chosen a lonely, dangerous path didn't escape her. But was it really a choice? Lorry and Charles were in danger because of her, and somehow, she had to make this right.

"Michelle, is something wrong with your grouper?"

She loaded her fork. "It's wonderful."

"You aren't eating."

"I'm tired," she said. "This has been a long, hard day, and I'm disappointed we didn't find Lorry and Charles."

"We'll find them. Tomorrow I'll check out a few things that should at least give us a direction to look in. Eleanor may be able to think of something."

Familiar, who'd managed to slip in with them, was under the table. Lucas had been feeding him shrimp, and Michelle put some of the fish on a small saucer and slipped it to him. She was rewarded with a sandpapery kiss on her shin, a sensation that almost made her giggle. Heaven forbid that the cat find out she was ticklish.

"Listen, Michelle, this will end okay."

She wanted to believe him, but it was difficult. Ever since the gallery exhibit had opened, she'd felt as if she'd stepped into a nightmare. Things didn't turn out okay in nightmares. They just got worse.

Lucas was staring at her. She wanted to meet his gaze with bravado, but she found she couldn't. She wasn't normally dishonest by nature, and the fact that she was going to deceive him left her feeling cheap and low. Her hand strayed to her purse, but she'd already surreptitiously checked it twice. Lucky she'd thought to pack the prescription sleeping pills, which she rarely took.

"I'm sorry you got mixed up in this. I know it was an innocent mistake."

She lifted a shoulder. Why was he being so nice now? It was only going to make what she had to do harder than ever.

She felt the cat's sharp claws in her thigh, and she almost jumped, but she controlled herself. "I'm sorry, too, Lucas," she said. "If I could undo it, I would."

"I believe you."

When she looked at him, her breath caught in her chest. He was staring at her as if he really saw her, saw beyond the physical and into her very heart. She'd never experienced such a thing. All through her childhood, she'd wanted someone to really see her, and now that it was happening, she felt panic.

"Do you want to leave?" Lucas asked. He was putting his napkin on the table.

"No!" She ate a forkful of her fish. "This is the best seafood I've ever had. Let's finish our meal. Besides, Familiar would never forgive me if I forced him to leave before he got his fill. He thinks we're starving him."

"Who would've thought a cat could be so…articulate," Lucas said. He reached across the table for the salt as her fingers circled the crystal shaker.

The warmth of his hand was like a promise, a vow of protection from a man who was solid and real. They both froze. She saw his throat work as he swallowed, and she felt the flush of blood move along her skin. The merest touch of his hand had sent her into a tailspin.

Of all times, why, in this situation, was the one thing she'd dreamed of happening? She'd dated, both seriously and for fun. She'd been engaged and had broken it off when she discovered that her fiancé had problems with the truth. But with all the men she'd known, she'd never before felt such a rush of intimacy, such a driving desire for his hand on her flesh.

The merest brush of his fingers sent a sensual thrill through her from head to toe. Her body was alive in a way it had never been before. Lucas, too, was affected. She could see it in the shallowness of his breathing and the way his gray eyes seemed to drink her in.

"More wine?" the waiter asked, breaking the moment.

Michelle pushed the salt into Lucas's hand. She felt disoriented.

"Michelle, would you like more?"

She shook her head. "I'm already a little dizzy. I don't think more would be a good idea." It wasn't the wine that had sent her head spinning, and she knew it.

"Just the check," Lucas said.

Familiar eased from beneath the tablecloth, stretched and jumped into the seat beside Michelle. His wise gold-green eyes read far too much, and Michelle found herself blushing anew.

Even if she could call Marco or Kevin, neither would believe that she was embarrassed because a cat had witnessed her pass the salt to a man. Jiminy, she was losing it. Really losing it.

LUCAS TOOK THE SALT AS if he didn't know what it was. The touch of Michelle's hand had been unexpected. He'd been kicked by a mule once as a young boy, and the impact had been less. Michelle Sieck was a dangerous woman. He'd underestimated her. He wouldn't make that mistake again.

Until this was resolved, he'd make certain that their fingertips didn't so much as graze each other. Once this was behind them, though, and if Michelle had to be put into the witness protection program, he might decide to reapply for his badge. Or he might start a private bodyguard service. The idea made him smile. To hide his thoughts from her, he focused on his food.

Whatever was happening in that pretty little head of hers, she didn't have much of an appetite. The cat had eaten most of her fish.

Well, they'd get a hotel room. His thoughts hit that spot and ground to a stop. They'd have to share a room. There was no way he could allow her to stay by herself. Not even with the cat. Michelle was a woman who acted on impulse, and that could be a dangerous thing.

He stabbed another bite of shrimp, trying to come up with a solution. This was one battle he didn't look forward to, but it was one he couldn't afford to lose.

LITTLE MISS SHUTTERBUG ACTS like she's got ants in her pants. Which tells me she's up to something. And Lucas is becoming so besotted with her that he can't see it. Which means that before the night is over, my incredible skills will be called into play.

Even from under the table, I can watch the interaction between the two of them. I peep at him, and he's staring at her. I peep at her, and she's toying with that heavenly fish on her plate, but she won't look him in the eye.

These are not teenagers on a first date. This

is a U.S. marshal and an NYC professional. Not exactly your shy and retiring types. But the crosscurrent of desire is so strong, I'm glad to stay under the table. I'm afraid the electrical charge would blast me out of my sleek black fur coat.

What Lucas is missing, though, is the guilt stamped clearly on Miss Shutterbug's face. She's hot and bothered, but that's physical. She's so miserable, she can't eat. My prediction is that she's feeling the pinch of something she's about to do, not a past deed.

So, I'll kick back here under the table and enjoy the last of this sumptuous seafood and see what happens.

There's her hand going into her purse. Is she deliberately being sly, or is she simply checking for her lipstick? The former, of course.

And what does she bring forth from the depths of that bag but a prescription. Hand in lap, she's fumbling the top off. It's possible that she has a medical condition and is only taking her meds, but I'm not nearly that naive. I've been around too many humanoids to buy that for one second.

And Lucas is standing up, going to the gentlemen's room, I presume. And there her hand is, moving up, up, and she's leaning across the table.

A little claw right in the old calf muscle, and she's letting out a shriek like she found a snake in her shoes. Here comes Lucas on the double-quick. And she's laughing and pretending that she startled herself.

Ha-ha, very funny. He's buying her story. And my goodness, he just gulped down his glass of wine in one swallow—along with whatever she put in it.

Chapter Seven

To Lucas's surprise, Michelle didn't argue about the room. She got her bag out of the rental car and claimed one of the double beds. Within moments, she was in the bathroom, brushing her teeth and preparing for the night. He figured she was as exhausted as he was. Suddenly, he could barely hold his eyes open. Several sleepless nights in a row had finally caught up with him.

He piled up the pillows on his bed and leaned back into them, waiting for his turn in the bathroom. He had to chuckle at the black cat. Familiar had perched atop Michelle's overnight bag and was watching the bathroom door like he figured the bogeyman would come through it.

He had to admit, the cat was a trip. He'd give Eleanor a call first thing in the morning and let her know the feline was safe and gaining his respect.

Lucas yawned, his eyes sliding shut before he could even brush his teeth. Struggling into a sitting position, he felt the room begin to spin.

This wasn't right! He'd had only two glasses of wine. He was tired, sure, but not tired enough to be dizzy.

He got his feet on the floor and tried to stand, but his legs wouldn't support him. Tottering, he felt back onto the bed. Now his arms and legs wouldn't respond at all.

Panic made him flounder, but no amount of mental willfulness could force his body to respond.

He knew then what had happened. Michelle had put something in his wine. And she was hiding out in the bathroom, waiting for it to take effect.

When he came out of this, he was going to find some handcuffs and keep her confined. Just as soon as…

MICHELLE PEEKED INTO THE room. Lucas was sprawled across the bed. She could see where he'd tried to get up and failed.

She opened the door and stepped to the bed. The cat was on top of her bag and refused to budge. His little way of showing that he disapproved of her actions.

"I have to do this," she told him, feeling only slightly ridiculous for explaining herself to a cat. "This mess is all my fault. I have to find Lorry and unite her with Lucas so he can keep her safe. Then I'll get the Maxims to chase me. It's the only way I can make this right."

To her surprise, Familiar moved off her bag and let her repack her things. She picked up the car keys from the bedside table. Taking the rental car would mean leaving Lucas without a vehicle, but he was a man with resources. He'd get another car.

And he'd be furious.

She mentally cringed at that thought, but she would be gone. If her plan worked out, she'd send Lorry and Charles to the hotel to get Lucas, and she'd be headed west, toward Texas, dragging the Maxim organization behind her.

Lucas and Lorry could head in any other direction and be safe. Or at least safer.

Bag in hand, she stood near the door of the hotel room. Lucas looked so vulnerable, his boots still on the floor. She put her bag down and picked up his feet, trying to arrange him in a more comfortable position.

Her hand lingered on his shin. There was something about him that moved her. Had circumstances been different, she would have dated him, or at least hoped that he would ask her for a date. She wanted to know more about him, about what made him tick. In many ways, he was a contradiction, a mystery that piqued her interest on many levels.

This action she'd taken would forever destroy any chance of knowing him in any light other than that of an adversary.

Before she could stop herself, she placed a kiss on his forehead and then headed out the door. She threw her bag in the backseat and got behind the wheel.

She'd checked the directions, and Interstate 10 East would take her to the turn off for Gulf Shores. Within an hour, she'd find the address listed in the brochure. If Lorry and Charles were there, she'd alert them to the danger they faced and send them to Lucas so they could find safety.

It wasn't a great plan, but it was a whole lot better than sitting around waiting for the Maxims to strike.

THE CONDO WAS INCREDIBLE. A glass front gave a view of the waves, which rushed to the shore with a gentle whispering sound. Even in the dark, Michelle could imagine the beauty. She stood at the door, knocking loudly.

No one answered, and the first finger of

doubt traced along her spine. She was about to try the door when she felt something on her ankles. Startled, she looked down to find Familiar gazing up at her.

"How did you—" No point in asking that question. She knew the answer. He'd stowed away in the car, managing to get in and hide in the backseat. He was a clever kitty.

She turned the knob, and the door opened soundlessly. Stepping inside, she closed the door, blocking out the sound of the gulf. For a moment she simply stood, letting her eyes adjust to the gloom. Outside, a series of floodlights had illuminated the landing. Inside, though, the condo was quiet and in near darkness.

If Lorry and Charles were here, they were either asleep—unlikely with the front door unlocked—or… She pushed that thought aside and entered the den of the condo unit. The first thing she noticed was a smashed coffee table. Wooden splinters were strewn across the plush carpeting.

Heart pounding, she moved slowly through the kitchen.

"Meow!"

The cat's strident yowl made the hair on her neck lift in anticipation of something terrible.

"Me-ow!"

Whatever he'd found, the cat was adamant that she see it, too.

She followed his voice to the bathroom. As soon as she snapped on the light, she gasped. Blood streaked one wall. Fresh blood. Or at least not-so-old blood. She wasn't a forensic expert, so she couldn't tell for certain, but it was smeared across the tiles of the shower. Surely if it wasn't fresh, someone would have washed it off.

Unless that someone wasn't able to wash anything!

She stifled the small cry of fear and backed into the hallway, finding support against one wall.

The Maxims had beat her to the condo. If she'd been able to find the brochure, so had they. The men who meant to kill Lorry were one step ahead at every turn.

"What should we do?" she asked the cat. Too bad if a psychiatrist would likely commit her for asking a cat for advice. Familiar had discovered the blood. Maybe he knew what she should do about it.

"Meow." The cat walked calmly down the hallway and to the bedroom.

She followed, because she didn't know what else to do. When he used his paws to pitter-patter against the closed bedroom door, she knew what he wanted. The thing she dreaded doing—looking inside the bedroom. What if Lorry and Charles were in there, dead?

And what if they were hurt?

Standing outside the door, wasting time, could cost them their lives.

She pushed the door open and flipped the light on. The bedroom was pristine. Sighing, she realized there was nowhere else in the house for Lorry to be.

"What now?"

"Meow." Familiar was obviously in his element since she'd turned over control to him. He went to the front door, scratched to get out, and then sauntered along the cement balcony to the next door neighbor's. Looking at her as if the solution were obvious, he pawed at that door.

"Okay, okay." She followed up with a loud knock. The cat was right. Canvassing the neighbors was exactly what would happen on one of the TV cop shows.

The door opened two inches, revealing a young woman who held a hand to the throat of her shirt, a gesture of apprehension.

Michelle gave her most winning smile. "I'm sorry to disturb you, but I'm looking for the couple who rented the condo next door. They're newlyweds, and I missed the wedding, but I have a gift for them."

The young woman visibly relaxed. "They were so cute," she said, a fleeting smile moving over her face. "So much in love." The frown returned. "What's going on with them?"

"I think they're in dan—" She snapped her mouth shut on the cry of pain that almost escaped. Familiar had dug both sets of front claws into the back of her thigh. "I mean, what are you talking about? Is something wrong?"

The woman edged the door open a little more and craned her head out to glance up and down the long balcony that ran across the front of the building. She caught sight of Familiar and smiled again. "What a beautiful cat. Is he yours?"

Michelle hesitated for only a fraction of a second. "He is. He's sort of my boss, in fact."

The woman glanced left and right again and then motioned Michelle closer. "Those men were scary."

Michelle schooled her features into a mask of confusion. "Men? What men?" The cat had let her know that she was there to obtain information, not give it out.

"Why should I tell you anything about this? You're not a cop." The woman's suspicion returned.

Michelle reached into her purse and pulled out her business card. "I met Lorry when I was doing a shoot for *Bride Magazine.* I need to find her."

The name of the magazine worked its magic. Almost every young woman had skimmed through the bridal shots at one point in her life. The door widened, and the woman looked around, as if to make sure Michelle was alone.

At last, the woman took a deep breath. "Come on in. I'll tell you everything I can. Something isn't right with Lorry and Charles. I haven't seen them since late this afternoon, when they took off. And then those men came, and there was all that racket, and then the police…"

Michelle felt her hopes sink, but she took a seat. She'd learn all she could and then decide what to do next. "You saw Lorry and Charles leave?"

The woman nodded. "I did. I had some wonderful muffins from a shop on the beach, but they were in such a hurry, they didn't even have time to say goodbye properly. I think someone in the family was very ill."

Michelle realized the black cat had slipped inside, too. He was in the shadows, inspecting the condo, checking for God knew what.

"Did Lorry happen to mention where she might be going, Mrs.….?"

"Just call me Lidell." The woman shook her

head. "No, she never said. She's from this area. I could tell by the accent. But she never said where she was going. Probably wherever her family is from, if someone is sick."

The logic worked, but it wasn't correct. "What did the men look like?"

Lidell's eyes widened. "Oh, they were scary. Vile men in expensive suits. They got out of a black car, and one of them forced the door open. I saw it all through my window." She pointed to a bay window that would give an excellent view of the condo next door.

"Expensive suits and what else?"

"They were young. Midthirties or less. And one of them had a New York accent. I heard him talking. The others didn't talk much. He was the one giving orders, and I feel certain he was the one who hurt one of the other men."

Michelle remembered the blood and hoped it had belonged to one of Maxim's men and not to Lorry or Charles. "How do you know someone hurt one of the men?"

The woman leaned forward, her pale eyes wide. "I heard him scream. The New York man was so angry, he was shouting, and I could hear it through the wall. He said, 'You're nothing but a total—' uh, a bad word '—and I'm going to make you sorry for the day you were born.' I heard that clearly, and then I heard a man cry out in pain. There was a crash, like something heavy hitting the wall. That's when I called the police, but by the time they got here, those awful men were gone."

Michelle played the scene in her mind. It was clear that Robert Maxim didn't like to be disappointed. When someone crossed him in any way, they paid.

As Lorry would pay.

As she would pay.

If he caught either of them.

That was what she had to make certain didn't happen.

"Thanks, Lidell."

"You're welcome. I hope you find Lorry and Charles and that they're okay."

Michelle rose to her feet. Familiar waited patiently by the door. "If someone comes by here and asks if you've seen me, could you see your way clear to…fibbing a little?"

"Why should I fib?" she asked.

"Those men, they're dangerous. I don't know why they're bothering Lorry, but they are. I'm going to find her and make sure she's okay, but my life is a little complicated."

"What's this really all about?"

Michelle forced herself not to growl. Lidell was asking sensible questions. The problem was that she didn't have time to answer them.

"Let's just say that I owe Lorry. I made a big mistake, and I'm trying to make amends."

Lidell smiled. "I can tell a little white lie for you." She rose also. "Just take care of Lorry and Charles. They seem like real good people."

"You bet." Michelle went to the door. "I'll just leave Lorry a note in case she comes back."

Outside Lidell's condo, Michelle let the roar of the gulf wash over her. The water was loud, the surf foaming onto the beach. She was completely alone, and she was in way over her head.

The cat rubbed against her ankles, and she bent down to pick him up. Holding Familiar made her feel better. Cradling him, she opened the door of Lorry's condo and went back for a final check. She had to find out where the young woman had gone.

Chapter Eight

Lucas struggled against the blanket of darkness that engulfed him. He was in a dense fog. Something terrible lurked just outside his range of vision, obscured by the roiling layers of mist and the blackness. Still, he knew it was there. He felt it drawing closer, an evil menace that loomed.

Michelle, unaware of the danger and unprotected, was somewhere in the distance. He reached for her, but he grasped only emptiness. He had to save her, to keep her from the danger that lurked in the gray shadows.

At last he forced his eyes open. It required all his effort to turn his head to the left. What he saw only confused him more. The wall was covered in a brisk pattern of tans and creams, and the painting of two springer spaniels darting through the woods was so unfamiliar that he couldn't comprehend where it had come from.

It dawned on him at last that he was the element out of place in the room. He didn't belong there. And he tried to remember where he was and how he'd gotten there.

The bedside clock showed 10:20 p.m. He couldn't remember how much time had passed since he'd gone to sleep, yet he felt an urgent need to get moving. In answer to that anxiety, he pushed himself up on his elbows. He was fully clothed in bed in a strange motel room.

It took him a moment to connect the dots, but when he did, he felt a rush of anger so fierce and pure that it gave him a moment of clarity. He'd been bushwhacked by a New York City photographer. And when he caught up with her—and he would—she was going to be in serious trouble. He couldn't take her to jail, because he was no longer an officer of the law. But he could detain her until some deputies or marshals or even a dang game warden could be found to make the charges official.

Unless Robert Maxim found her first.

He forced his body off the bed. Wobbling, he reached for the wall for support. Somehow, though, the wall moved. He leaned toward it, going too far. His equilibrium was gone. He went down hard, his head striking the floor with a smack. Not even the carpet could protect him.

Lucas sprawled on the floor, swallowed yet again by the black void of unconsciousness.

MICHELLE CHECKED HER WATCH. It was nearly ten-thirty, and she was still at the condo. The night was slipping away from her, just like her lead from Lucas. The sleeping pills she'd given him wouldn't last forever. This was precious time when she'd hoped to put distance between them.

"Meow."

Familiar sat on his haunches at her feet. His gold-green eyes asked a question, but she didn't know how to interpret it.

"Me-ow." He reached a paw under the sofa and batted at something. Curious, Michelle dropped to her knees and lifted the skirt of the sofa.

She saw a metallic object, and with a silent prayer, she picked it up. Her fingers closed around the silver cell phone, and she pulled it out, clutching it tightly.

The condo was still in darkness. Turning on the light would advertise her presence there. It was possible the Maxim organization was still watching the condo in the hopes that Lorry and Charles would return.

If that was the case, she was a sitting duck. That thought made her sink to the floor, the sofa a good block against anyone who might shoot through the front window.

When her heart stopped pounding, she wanted to beat her head against a wall. She simply wasn't cut out for this kind of life. She'd hoped to help, but was she? If she got herself shot to pieces, it wouldn't do much good.

Worse than that was the image Lucas had planted of torture. She had no illusions about herself. She'd tell them anything they wanted to know, even if she had to make it up. She didn't want to be hurt. It wasn't that she was deliberately courting danger for the thrill of it. Cowering on the floor was not her idea of a way to spend an evening.

Still, she flipped open the cell phone and punched the Call button. The last call made came up on the screen. She recognized the Dallas area code. She'd talked frequently with a magazine there that used her work.

Dallas was the home of Robert Maxim. She's heard Lucas say it more than once. The men who'd been in the condo were Robert's men. This cell phone was likely a direct link to the gangster.

Closing her eyes, she held the phone and tried to think of the best thing to do. *Call Lucas* instantly sprang into her head, but she couldn't. He was still under the influence of the sleeping pills. Once he regained his faculties, he wasn't going to be in a mood to hand out help to her.

She had no way of getting in touch with Lorry. The last option was the only viable one.

She pressed the Call button and listened as the phone began to ring.

"Hello." The male voice that answered was guarded.

"I know where Lorry Kennedy has gone, Mr. Maxim." She spoke clearly and was proud that her voice didn't tremble.

"And why would I be interested in her?" the man asked.

He didn't deny that he was Robert Maxim. Michelle visualized him. Cold, cunning, slightly eager because he thought his prize had been dropped in his lap. Once he heard the rest of it, he was going to be very angry.

"I know you're hunting for her."

"You claim to know a lot for an anonymous caller."

"I know I'm calling from a cell phone that belongs to one of your men." She let that sink in.

"So you're clever. That could be useful in my organization."

"How useful?" She hadn't meant to ask that question, but it was logical, and she appeared eager. Maybe she could make him believe she was willing to sell information.

"Mid-six figures."

"I'd have to be very useful to earn that, wouldn't I?" She made her tone coy. Her heart rate had calmed a little. Robert Maxim was likely hours away. She wasn't in imminent danger.

"What do you have for me?" He'd grown tired of the game.

"A location for Lorry."

"Why should I believe you?"

"Because I'm calling voluntarily."

"That's a circumstance, not a reason. But go ahead. Tell me what you know."

"Are you kidding? And trust you to give me my money?"

Robert laughed. "You're all alike. You want to squeeze and squeeze. Just remember, I don't like being pushed into a corner."

His tone chilled her. "If you want Lorry, you're going to have to find me first." She slammed the phone shut.

"Me-e-e-ow!" Familiar was at the window, batting it with his paws.

Michelle's stomach dropped to her knees. While she'd been toying with Robert, hoping to make him so angry at her that he forgot about Lorry and Lucas, it was probable that he'd been signaling his minions. They'd know exactly where to look for her and the damn telephone.

In fact, they could be sitting outside the condo right this moment. Just because she'd dialed a Dallas area code didn't mean Robert had to be in Dallas. She might have called a cell phone; she'd never considered that.

She wasn't half as smart as she'd thought she was.

"Familiar!" She called the cat as she pressed 9-1-1 on the cell phone. As soon as an operator answered, she gave her location. "Men are trying to kill me," she said.

When she hung up, she put the phone in her pocket and hurried to the bathroom. She'd noticed a window. Pushing it open, she called the cat. Before he could protest, she dropped him outside and climbed after him.

She hit the ground with a soft thud, falling onto the silky sand. From the condo came the sound of a door crashing open. Bullets sprayed the walls.

Before she could even think, she was running to the rental car, the cat at her side.

GOOD GRIEF. I HAVEN'T been shot at in a while, but Miss Shutterbug is doing her best to make sure we come as close to death as possible. She has to realize that she isn't blessed with nine lives like I am. It would behoove her to use a little more care.

I heard her talking to that Maxim thug, and I honestly didn't believe my ears. The girl has got a set of brass... Excuse me, I shouldn't even think such things in polite company. Let's just say she's not lacking in courage, but her good sense is in short supply.

At last we made it to the car. I can see those men in the open doorway of the condo.

And thank goodness, here come the police. Blue lights have never looked better. Ah, the bad guys are scattering. There they go, tires squealing, and the cops are after them. Now's our chance to get in the car and get away from here.

We don't want to be caught by the bad guys, and we sure as heck don't want to be picked up by the police, though they might know Lucas.

That's what we should do. We should go find Lucas. Michelle is too hardheaded to admit that she needs him. In fact, I think she's more afraid of needing Lucas than she is of Robert Maxim. That tells me she's got a big old wound that's in the driver's seat of her life. I've got more hair than Dr. Phil, but I'm just as fast at diagnosing emotional issues.

Okay, so we're on the road. That's good. And I see the bay sparkling in the starlight in front of us. So we're headed west. I wish she'd let me steer. I'd take us straight to Lucas. But since that isn't going to be the case, I guess I'll just curl up and take a nap. As soon as she stops again, I'm sure she'll need me to keep her from getting her butt shot off. Geez, Miss Shutterbug is a whole lot of woman and a whole lot of work.

LUCAS AWOKE TO A RINGING telephone. His cell phone. He found it, feeling the pounding of a fierce headache as he pushed himself off the floor.

"Hello."

"Lucas, it's Frank."

His ex-partner's voice was a welcome surprise. "Frank, why are you calling?"

"Where the heck are you, man? We picked up a report from the local sheriff's office in Baldwin County, Alabama. There was an attempted murder in a condo unit rented by Charles and Lorry Kennedy—our only witness against Antonio Maxim."

Lucas sat down on the edge of the bed. "When?"

"Last night, about ten-thirty. That was the second call for the local sheriff's department. They'd been there once before, on a call from a neighbor about a fight between some dangerous-looking men. Lorry's new handler tried to contact her, but she's not responding. What the heck is going on?"

"There's trouble, Frank. I lost the photographer." Lucas gave him a thumbnail account of events. "The photographer slipped me a Mickey." He felt like a fool confessing it. He'd been sitting across the table from her, watching the candlelight in her hair, the play of shadows on her creamy skin. He'd been an idiot.

"Captain Wells is going to be upset. What are you going to do? Have you heard from the witness?"

"Nothing. She's on the run. She must know she's in danger, and Lorry's smart. She's a survivor."

"And this photographer? What about her?"

He wanted to say that when he found her, he'd wring her neck, but he bit back the words. The redhead had frustrated him at every turn. She'd invaded his dreams, making him worry even when he'd been drugged. Besides, he'd never been one to make idle threats. "I'll find her."

"It gets worse. Maxim's lawyer is asking for an expedited appeal. He wants to push it through in two days. We have to have Lorry at that hearing."

"I know." The Maxims were smart and deadly. They'd killed his brother in cold blood, knowing he was a police officer. It had been calculated, a clear message to anyone else who tried to interfere in their business.

Frank sighed. "We'll send a team down there."

"This is something I need to handle on my own."

"You're not a marshal any longer, Lucas. You can't handle this."

Lucas swallowed. "Lorry never trusted anyone but me. You know that. I can find her and get her to that hearing. I'm not sure anyone else can."

"Damn it, Lucas. Without her testimony, Antonio walks."

"I'm aware of that, Frank. Antonio killed my brother, remember."

There was a hum on the line before Frank spoke again. "Call me if you need anything. And stay in touch."

"You bet." Lucas ended the call. He was torn. He had to assume that Lorry and Michelle were headed in different directions. What course of action would draw the Maxims away from Lorry? As much as he hoped to protect Michelle, Lorry was his priority. She'd sacrificed everything to get justice for his brother.

Chapter Nine

The sun rose above the tops of the pine trees, causing the dew-soaked grass to sparkle. Michelle yawned and sat up in the car. Her body was sore and achy, the result of sleeping in a cramped position on the car seat. Beside her, Familiar batted the door handle to let her know he needed out.

That was fine for him. There were woods everywhere. But she needed running water, a hot shower, and a bathroom. She'd never slept in a car. This wasn't the life she aspired to.

She'd driven for a couple of hours in sheer terror. The attack by Maxim's henchmen had brought home the foolishness of her conduct. Yet she couldn't turn back. She couldn't simply quit. She'd set this in motion, and she had to try to do something to make it right.

She watched Familiar head into the woods and then return. Good grief. When he got back in the car, he gazed at her, and she thought for a moment that she saw disappointment. Well, he had a right to be disappointed in her. They were both starving. She had a flash of what Marco and Kevin would say if they could see her. If the situation wasn't so dangerous, it would be funny.

She started the car and drove out of the woods on a search for food. Even in the wilderness, people had to eat. And speaking of wilderness, she'd never seen such vast stretches of trees. The asphalt road wound into the distance, a gray whisper that was lost in the darkness of the woods.

Where was she? Since she didn't have a map, she didn't have a clue. The only thing she knew was that she'd followed Interstate 65 North across what was marked as the Mobile-Tensaw Delta. She'd driven another forty miles before she'd taken an exit and found herself in an isolated area.

But she'd passed a restaurant, and that was where she was going. There was no possible way the Maxims had been able to track her. She was safe enough to have some breakfast and wash her face in the bathroom.

"How about some bacon and eggs?" she asked the cat.

"Meow."

Funny, but it sounded exactly as if he'd said, "You bet." She stroked his head as she drove along the quiet road and back to the parking lot of Beulah's Diner.

Even though it was just after six in the morning, two dozen vehicles crowded the small parking lot. When she pushed open the door, a bell jangled and several men looked up at her. She'd had no experience with men dressed in overalls, but she guessed them to be farmers. Others in khakis and suits were probably local businessmen.

She was distinctly out of her element, but she ignored the curious looks and went to a small booth. Familiar had slipped in beside her. It would likely be difficult to explain the cat, but she wasn't going to eat without him.

A waitress with a name tag that read Donna showed up, pad and pencil in hand.

"Coffee?"

"Please," she said.

"That your Seeing Eye cat?" Donna asked.

"Yes. He is. He navigates and I drive."

Donna's laughter was rich. "That's a good one. Beulah isn't here, or she'd throw him out. Health department violation and all. But what she doesn't know won't hurt her."

"Heavy cream for the cat," Michelle said. Smiling back at Donna, she felt for the first time in what seemed like ages that maybe things might be okay.

Donna returned with her coffee and cream. "Turn the latch on the bathroom door so that it locks good, and you can wash up a little. I'll keep an eye on the cat while you're cleaning up. And I'll put your order in. By the time you come back, the food should be on the table."

"Give me the works," Michelle said. She could eat a cooked pigeon she was so hungry. "And give the cat some…"

"We have some leftover catfish. Delicious. I never met a cat who could turn down Beulah's fried fish."

Michelle smiled. "Perfect."

Familiar was lapping the cream as she hurried into the ladies' room to do the best she could to straighten herself up.

Deputy Mark Bewley let Lucas into the condo. Lucas examined the scene, stifling his twinge of conscience at the fact that he was impersonating a U.S. marshal and taking advantage of a young deputy's naiveté. As he did a cursory check of the condo, he made the same deductions that the Baldwin County deputies had made. Someone had forced their way through the front door, spraying bullets, while their quarry had escaped out the bathroom window.

According to the deputy, the blood in the bathroom was the result of a prior incident—after Lorry had left the condo and before Michelle arrived. Looking at it, Lucas felt relief. From what he could tell, Michelle hadn't been injured. And he had no doubt that it was Michelle who'd made her getaway through the window. Lidell, a talkative neighbor, had identified Michelle and even talked about her career as a photographer.

She'd also positively identified Lorry as the woman who'd rented the condo and disappeared before Michelle arrived.

Whatever the redhead was up to, she was making no attempt to disguise who she was.

And that bothered him. He suspected Michelle was using herself as bait. That could ultimately result in grave injuries and possibly death.

Michelle was just smart enough to get herself in serious trouble if she didn't watch out.

"We matched some of the prints we took in here," the deputy said. "Couple of thugs out of Texas. You know anything about that?"

How much to tell? "I do," he said. "Those are hired guns for Antonio and Robert Maxim. Antonio was convicted of capital murder for killing a Dallas police officer working undercover in New York. Antonio's appeal is coming up, and a witness in the case against him was staying in this condo." He kept it all business— only the bare facts. He couldn't afford for the Baldwin County Sheriff's Department to view him as a brother set on vengeance.

The deputy nodded. "How does the photographer fit into all this?"

Lucas wanted to sigh, but he didn't. "Accidental involvement. Wrong place, wrong time."

"That's tough."

Lucas nodded. "Yeah, it is. If you get any leads on where either the witness or the photographer might have gone, please notify me." He gave his cell phone number. "Both women are in danger."

"We've got an APB out on the rental car. We'll check into the DMV records to find out what the witness was driving."

Those were the basic beginning steps, but Lucas had to take action now. "Thanks. I appreciate the help."

"When a marshal says he's on special assignment, we take notice," the deputy said.

It was only a little white lie that Frank Halcomb had helped him pull off, while diverting Lorry's new case handler. The problem was that it put Frank in a bad position; he was lying, too, and Frank still had a career to wreck. But without the facade of law enforcement authority, Lucas would never have been allowed into the condo, and he certainly wouldn't get any assistance in finding Lorry or Michelle. Truth be told, he'd probably be sent packing back to Texas. And he couldn't let that happen. Time was critical. Antonio's appeal loomed. Lorry's life hung in the balance. He'd promised her she would be safe. He'd promised his brother that his killer would pay. And he kept his word. Though one redheaded female photographer was doing everything in her power to prevent him from doing so.

Lucas followed the deputy out of the condo and went to the new rental car. Frank had rented him a second vehicle because the first one had not been returned. Another reason for him to be furious with Michelle.

Instead, he was worried. The hot anger had cooled, and he was left with deep anxiety. For Michelle and for Lorry.

He placed a call to the gallery owner in SoHo, hoping that Michelle had tried there. He had to find her, put her someplace safe, so he could focus totally on Lorry's safety and getting her to New York for the appeal.

Marco answered on the third ring, and Lucas explained that he was calling on Michelle's behalf.

"Where is she? We've been worried sick," Marco said. "It isn't like Michelle to disappear, especially not when her photos have just been hung. I've called the magazine. No one has seen or heard from her."

"I was hoping she'd called you."

"No. Not a word. Ever since those men came by this morning, I've been terribly upset."

"What men?"

"They were undercover police or something. They said it was urgent they find Michelle."

Lucas took a breath. "Did they show you any credentials?"

There was a pause. "I didn't ask, and they didn't offer. They knew about Michelle and the exhibit, and the fiasco with that wedding picture."

"Did you show them the photograph of the bride?" Lucas couldn't be certain what clues were hidden in that picture. It was imperative the Maxims not be allowed to study it.

"Absolutely not! They said they'd come back with a warrant, and I told them to do so, but until I saw the warrant, I refused to let them look at the photograph."

"That's good, but you may have put yourself in harm's way. Those men weren't federal agents. They're criminals, and they have no boundaries. They'll use whatever force is necessary to attain their goal, and you have to know that you've stepped right into their path."

"Michelle is in trouble, isn't she?" Marco was agitated. "That's why the bride didn't want her picture hung or put in the magazine. Oh, my goodness, what has Michelle gotten herself into?"

"Let's just say that it's dangerous. You need to get rid of that photograph. Now." Lucas could see the Maxims torching the photo gallery in an act of revenge. They'd ruled through fear for so long, it was second nature to them.

"Get rid of it how?" Marco asked.

"Take it to the district attorney's office. Tell them it relates to the capital murder case of Harry West."

"West? Isn't that your name?"

"He was my brother."

"I'm so sorry," Marco said. "I'll do what you say."

"And if Michelle should call you, urge her to get in touch with me. I can protect her."

"Oh, my," Marco said. "Michelle is difficult. She has the idea that she has to be this tower of strength. She's never been able to rely on anyone else."

"She's making my job a lot harder than it has to be."

"I know," Marco said. "It's just that her parents… Well, let's say they don't approve of anything about her. Any success she has is a fluke, and any failure is what they expect and seem to relish."

"So you're telling me that she wouldn't call her parents if she were in trouble."

"If hell froze over."

"Give me their number. You know that, but the Maxim brothers don't. Michelle's parents could be their next target."

WITH HER FACE WASHED AND her belly full, Michelle felt infinitely better. Familiar snoozed in the sun on the passenger seat of the little car, and she tooled down the highway, wondering what to do next.

There was no sign of the Maxims. She still had the cell phone, and while the cat was asleep, she pulled it out. With the food, her nerve had returned. It was time for another taunting phone call.

One eye on the road and the other on working the phone, she was about to make the call when Familiar reached out a paw and knocked the phone from her hand.

"Hey!" She frowned at him. "That was rude, even for a bossy cat."

Familiar only gazed at her, and she had the

distinct sense that his judgment of her mental abilities was not kind.

The phone had fallen underneath her foot and the accelerator. The road was empty, and she slowed to a near stop before she reached down to fumble for it.

Slippery and difficult to grasp, the phone eluded her.

She cut loose with a string of curse words, which brought a slap on the back of her head from the cat. Stung, she lifted her head in time to see a car speeding toward her.

Familiar jumped at the steering wheel, wrenching it to the right and sending the rental car careering toward a ditch, narrowly avoiding the oncoming car.

Michelle struggled to bring the vehicle to a stop. The cell phone had slipped beneath the brake pedal, blocking it. With a kick, she sent the phone out of the way, stood on the brakes and stopped the car.

As she watched the speeding car depart in the rearview mirror, she heard sirens in the distance. Surely not in response to her near accident. Law enforcement couldn't have arrived so quickly. Not here, on the back side of nowhere.

She'd just pulled the car back onto the asphalt when she heard a dozen loud pops, like firecrackers.

She hesitated. In the rearview mirror, she saw sheriff's deputies take cover behind their two vehicles as the car that had nearly run her off the road careened past them. A man hung out the window, a gun extended as he fired at the deputies.

Michelle didn't wait around to see the outcome. She pressed the gas pedal to the floor and pointed the little car north, away from the confrontation. She had to get a map and figure out the back roads. She had no doubt that Lucas had alerted all the area law enforcement agencies to be on the lookout for her. But that wasn't her biggest concern. Men with guns were far more worrisome.

It was time to ditch the rental car and find something else to drive.

There was a place she could go! At the memory, she brightened. When she was fourteen, she'd demanded to be sent to an arts camp in the small town of Reba, Alabama. Her interest even then had been photography, and she'd spent eight summer weeks with master photographers who'd treated her with respect. It had been a summer that changed her life, because someone had finally believed in her.

She couldn't be certain, but she felt as if she were near Camp Imagine. If she could get there, maybe someone would help her. Either hide her or give her another vehicle.

It was worth a shot.

Chapter Ten

"I knew this photography foolishness would come to a bad end."

Lucas couldn't believe what he was hearing from Michelle's mother. He'd never been stunned into silence before.

"Michelle was a brilliant child. Brilliant. She had scholarships to engineering programs and medical schools. Everyone wanted her. But she chose to be a photographer." Mrs. Sieck said the word as if it tasted bad.

"Has she called you?" Lucas asked.

"Are you some kind of bill collector? Is Michelle in financial trouble? We told her, her father and I, that working in a field like photography would be living on pauper's wages. There's no guarantee in that kind of business."

"I'm a mar…a friend, ma'am, and I need to know if you've spoken with Michelle lately."

His harsh tone was met with complete silence.

Then Mrs. Sieck said, "Michelle hasn't broken the law. She's a willful young woman, but she isn't a criminal."

"Nothing like that. I merely need to speak with her. Has she been in contact with you?" Lucas wanted to bang the telephone against his forehead.

"She hasn't called here. But that's not unusual. She treats us like we have leprosy."

He could have said that he understood why, but he didn't. "If anyone should approach you for information about Michelle, please tell them nothing. These are dangerous men. Don't provoke them, and don't tell them anything about yourself or your daughter. I'll speak to the police in your jurisdiction and see about having someone sent out to guard you."

"What kind of joke is this?"

"I assure you, ma'am, this isn't a joke."

"Guard us! What kind of danger are we in?"

"Serious." It was all Lucas had the time, or patience, to explain. "Officers will be there soon. Until then, stay inside and don't open the door to anyone." He thought of several other things that he'd like to tell them—none very nice—but he restrained himself. He wasn't an officer of the law any longer, but he still had the sense that his conduct would reflect back on a group of law officers who deserved only respect.

He drove to the Baldwin County courthouse to see if the Alabama authorities had been able to track Michelle or Lorry. He'd left the wild beauty of the Mobile River Delta behind for the small town of Bay Minette. He drove down the unfamiliar highways, Michelle and Lorry heavy on his mind. Michelle was alone in a place she didn't know, with killers likely on her trail. If they caught her... That didn't bear thinking about.

Lorry was smarter, more street savvy, and she had Charles to assist her. Her new handler was doing everything he could to trace her through the marshals network. She'd success-fully covered her trail, but for how long? Robert Maxim was desperate to save his brother, Antonio. He'd kill Lorry without batting an eye. She was his first priority, but Michelle was still in the area. He had to find her quickly.

Talking with Marco and her parents had given him a unique view of her behavior. While he'd thought she was spoiled and undisci-plined, he now saw another picture. Her parents' constant criticism had forged her spirit into one of hardheadedness, but only to survive. No child could face parental rejection unless he or she toughened up. Michelle had clung to her independence and her dreams against the emotional assault of her parents.

Had she become a doctor or engineer, he wondered if that would have finally pleased them. He doubted it.

His childhood had been so different. He'd worked alongside his father and Harry every day. When the ranch chores were done, they'd gone to the house, where his mother met them with a smile, eager to hear the stories of fencing and cows saved from bogs or illness or birth. When the desire to bring justice to people had sent both brothers into law enforcement, his parents had supported their decision.

Instead of belittling him, his parents had worked hard to give him a sense of himself as a man, a man who knew right from wrong and who could handle himself.

He was still angry with Michelle because of the foolish risks she'd taken, but he understood better the reasons why. She felt she'd started all of this, and now she was going to pay the consequences and fix things if she could.

What she didn't understand was that Robert and Antonio Maxim had started this long ago, when they'd preyed upon vulnerable young girls who dared to dream of being models or movie stars. Sure the girls were naive and unrealistic, but they were children. And in some ways they were like Michelle—bold enough to act upon the dreams they harbored. They'd fallen into the wrong hands, though. And that could so easily have happened to Michelle, too. Could still happen.

The Maxims and their organization had robbed the girls of their innocence and their childhood, of their health and their futures, of their self-respect and even their lives.

Antonio was in jail, and hopefully he would soon pay with his life. And Robert?

A cold resolve clutched Lucas's heart. Robert was going to pay big-time, and if he harmed Michelle or Lorry, he would pay on the spot. He wouldn't get an opportunity to play the justice system as Antonio had.

MICHELLE SAW THE SIGN for the camp and pulled over. There was no traffic on the road in either direction, but she wanted a moment to accept the inevitable. The sign, once a thing of artistic beauty, was falling apart. It hung askew from a leaning post. Camp Imagine, Where Young People Find Their Dreams.

Her potential haven was abandoned. Her hopes sank to the floorboard. Somehow, she'd expected to find this place and drive back in time. When she'd been fourteen and come here, this had been the first place she'd ever felt valued for who she was and her talent to see light in a particular way.

As foolish as it might have been, she'd thought that if she could find Camp Imagine, she could find that place of security yet again. That was the reasoning of a child. Somehow, though, she needed to find safety, even if it was just a momentary respite.

The black cat put his front feet on the dash and examined the scene. He gave her a look as if to say, "This is where we're going to be safe?"

A lone pickup passed. Michelle recognized one of the older men from the café. He stared at her as he drove by and then waved. She returned the gesture and waited for him to disappear.

"It may work out for the best that no one is there. At least I won't be endangering anyone." Michelle turned down the gravel road and headed toward the camp. There had been cabins and picnic sites, a cafeteria, bathhouses and a big lake. In memory the place was huge. As she drove into the clearing, she saw what a trick her memory had played on her. Camp Imagine was tiny, a small compound nestled among towering pine trees.

Familiar clawed at the car door. She leaned over and opened it to let him out. He sauntered around, sniffing the air like a dog and walking the perimeter. Whoever he was, he was a very special creature.

She walked to the edge of the lake, fighting the disappointment that wanted to paralyze her. The place was peaceful and serene.

While the lake was smaller than she remembered, it was clear and inviting. She ached for a bath. The washup in the café had taken care of her face, but she needed a full, all-over cleaning.

She grabbed her bag from the car and went down to the water's edge. In a moment she was in the water, swimming hard, burning off the fear and frustration that had settled in all her limbs.

So far, her plan had failed utterly. She had accomplished nothing. And she was out of touch with everyone.

As soon as she got dressed, she would call Marco or Kevin. They'd check the news for her and see if anything about Lorry or Lucas had been reported.

Feeling better with a firm plan in mind, she flipped to her back and floated for a few moments in the bracingly cold water.

TENSION GRIPPED LUCAS'S shoulders as he talked into the phone. "None of the deputies were hit?"

He'd just been told about the shoot-out on a county road north of Mobile. Although the deputies were not hurt, the shooters had disabled the two patrol cars and escaped. And the deputies had spotted a car matching the description of the rental car Michelle was driving.

"Thanks so much, Officer." He closed the cell phone and turned his vehicle around. Michelle had been seen on a county road north of I-65, headed toward the town of Reba, Alabama.

Shortly after the shooting, a farmer on his way to round up some loose cattle had called the Monroe County Sheriff's Office because he'd seen Michelle parked beside the entrance to an old abandoned artists' camp. He couldn't stop to help, but he'd been concerned that her car had broken down, and had called for assistance for her.

She was no more than two hours away. Lucas had to catch up with her before Robert Maxim did.

As he drove, he placed a call to Frank. His ex-partner told him that there'd been no word from Lorry and no reports that anyone had seen her.

"You checked all the safe houses?" Lucas asked.

"Every one in the vicinity."

Lucas forced his grip on the phone to loosen. "Call me if you hear anything."

"Will do. And be careful."

Lucas put the phone on the seat and concentrated on his driving. What the heck was Michelle Sieck doing in the middle of the woods in Alabama? She didn't strike him as the kind of woman who wanted to camp, not even in an artists' community.

Suddenly he remembered one of the few facts she'd voluntarily revealed. A photographers' camp in the middle of the Alabama woods. It shouldn't be hard to find. Any local would know it.

He could only hope that she stayed there long enough for him to run her down.

MISS SHUTTERBUG IS A FULL-TIME guard job. She's out in that lake, flipping and cavorting as if she hasn't a care in the world. She never considered how humiliating it might be to be captured by the Maxim brothers in the buff.

Lucky for her, I'm on guard duty.

This is an interesting place, I have to say. I wonder how Michelle found her way here. I mean, a New York photographer and an abandoned arts camp for high school kids? Doesn't seem like much of a match to me.

Just another one of the little mysteries surrounding Michelle Sieck. She's a strange one, for sure. All that independence wrapped around a marshmallow center. The trouble is, the Maxims won't care if she's cream-filled or nuts. They'll kill her just the same.

She's been in that lake for an hour. She'll be all shriveled like a prune when she finally gets out. I mean, really. Water? And cold water at that! Bipeds have the most extraordinary ability to entertain themselves with unpleasant activities.

Take horseback riding. Don't get me wrong. I admire the noble equine and love to watch them buck and run in a green pasture. Riding is another matter. No reason in the world to climb aboard a horse when I have four perfectly good legs.

Or this swimming business. I mean, she's immersed in water. That says it all.

Now I could enjoy a nice soft pillow in a sunny window where I could watch the birds flitter by. Perhaps a dish of pan-seared grouper at my side. Some music playing, and lovely Clotilde snuggled up beside me. That is the kind of activity I find worthwhile.

Yet here I am, in the middle of Alabama, with a woman who thinks she's a dolphin. She does have a lovely breaststroke, but when all is said and done, she's going to drip all over me.

Uh-oh. I hear someone coming.

My attempts to alert Michelle are going

unheeded. No matter how loud I yowl, she can't hear me underwater.

Jeez Louise! It's up to me to set an ambush. Lucky for her, she has me to take care of her.

THE THICK COVER OF TREES opened up on the small campsite and the beautiful lake. Lucas saw the rental car instantly. Michelle and the cat were nowhere in evidence.

His heart rate spiked, and he drove slowly around the camping area, taking in the dilapidated old buildings, the air of decay that hung over the place. Still, it was beautiful.

Out of the corner of his eye, he saw movement. The black cat flashed between trees. Lucas almost smiled. Very slowly, he let his window down.

"Familiar, it's me."

The cat popped up twenty yards ahead of him. The little devil could move like lightning. And he was stalking Lucas.

He stopped the car and slowly got out, scanning for Michelle. If Familiar was here, it stood to reason Michelle was, too. The cat rushed up to rub against his legs.

"Glad to see me, are you?" Lucas said, easing down to stroke the cat's back. "Where is she?"

"Me-ow!" Familiar trotted toward the lake.

A flash of long legs broke the water with barely a splash, and Lucas knew he'd found Michelle. The crazy woman was swimming! He felt his temper rise. Who in her right mind would take a swim break when killers were on her trail?

He was totally unprepared for her when she surfaced and stood up.

She was absolutely, stunningly naked. Or *nekkid,* as they said in Texas.

She saw him and froze like a deer. Before he could utter a sound, she dove back into the water and disappeared.

Lucas felt the heat in his face. Not since high school had he felt like such a gawking fool. Standing at the edge of the lake, with his jaw hanging open like he'd never seen a nude woman before.

The truth was, he'd never seen one that looked like Michelle Sieck.

Chapter Eleven

When she could no longer hold her breath, Michelle surfaced far out in the lake. She treaded water as she rubbed her eyes clear and looked toward the shore. It hadn't been a hallucination. Lucas West was on the shore, his back discreetly turned to her.

"Michelle, come on out. I put your clothes on the bank."

Michelle wanted to swim in the opposite direction. But what was the point? Her clothes were there, beside the lawman. And while he would give her the necessary privacy to dress, he would not trust her a second time. She was well and truly caught.

She swam toward shore. When her feet could touch, she saw no other way. "I'm coming out."

"I'll wait right here."

"Could you at least move behind one of the buildings?"

He shook his head. "You're kidding, right? I just walk away so you can grab your clothes, hop in the car and take off again. No, way, lady."

Arguing was pointless. She slowly moved out of the water. Never in her life had she felt so totally vulnerable.

True to his word, Lucas kept his back turned.

"Talk to me," he said. "I have to hear your voice so I know where you are."

"What would you like me to say?" she asked, a bit of acid in her tone.

"How about 'Thanks, Lucas. You've just spent a day of your life trying to find me to keep me safe, and I really appreciate it.' That would be nice for starters."

"Dream on." But she did thank him, even if she couldn't bring herself to verbally express it. "Look, I feel bad about the sleeping pills." She pulled fresh clothes from her overnight bag and quickly began to dress.

"You should."

"I didn't want to involve you. And I wanted to find Lorry and help her."

"And what is it that you think I want to do? Find her and feed her to the Maxims?"

Irritation made his voice rough, and she responded with a hint of heat. "Of course not. But if those men are as dangerous as you say, then

I didn't want to put you… I wanted to fix this myself."

"Lady, you may be a great photographer, but as a strategist against mobsters and murderers, you need some training."

She jerked her blouse over her head. And just in time. He turned around as she pulled her hair free from her collar. His eyes were a gunmetal gray, and the intensity of his look made her catch her breath. He was furious with her, but it didn't stop the jolt that ran through her body. Lucas West was like grabbing a tornado and trying to hang on.

"Leave the rental here. I'll call and have it picked up. You're riding with me in the SUV," he ordered.

Furious with the hammer of her heart, she stood her ground. "I don't take orders. Not even from a former U.S. marshal." She realized as soon as the words left her mouth that she'd pushed the boundaries a little too hard. In one long step, he was beside her. His hand caught her wrist, and he snapped a pair of cuffs on her left arm.

Seemingly without effort, he scooped her up and carried her to the SUV. Before she could say "Jack Sprat," he'd cuffed her to the steering wheel.

"Take it easy, or take it hard," he said. "Either

way, you're going to do what I tell you. Not because I want to order you around, but because you're in danger. The best chance you have for surviving is to listen to me. If you're too pig-headed to do it because it makes sense, then you'll do it because you don't have another choice."

Michelle started to reply, but she clamped her teeth together and bit back the furious words. Lucas was too angry to reason with. And her problem was that she could see why. The day she'd walked into that church and taken those photographs of a woman who didn't want to be in a picture, she'd started a landslide of events that had wreaked havoc on Lucas's life and on the people he cared about.

So she settled back against the seat and kept her mouth shut.

Outside the vehicle, Lucas gathered Familiar into his arms. He was a lot gentler with the cat than he had been to her. Then again, Familiar hadn't screwed up.

He put Familiar in the backseat and slid into the front, forcing her to climb over the console.

"You aren't going to drive with me cuffed to the steering wheel, are you?" Now that was a recipe for screwing up.

He considered it. "I guess not." He unlocked the handcuff that was latched around the wheel.

In a quick movement, he attached it to his buckled seat belt. "There now. You happy?" he asked.

"You are a sadist," she said softly.

"And you are not going to give me the slip again. Whatever you do, I do with you."

"E-e-e-e-YOW!"

The cry came from the backseat just before a spray of bullets tore some of the glass from the SUV.

Michelle felt her head pushed down. Lucas started the vehicle and spun out, slinging mud behind him as the wheels finally gained purchase, and the big machine roared forward and into the side of the vehicle that had come so quietly down the secluded camp road.

"Damn it all to hell." Lucas backed up, rammed the car again, then reversed and sped around it. As they made the first curve, another spray of rapid gunfire took out the rear window of the vehicle.

Glass tinkled all around them, but Lucas didn't stop. Michelle kept her head down. She squinted her eyes shut and prayed. She'd never considered what it might feel like to be shot at twice in as many days. Lucas had warned her—repeatedly—that the Maxims were killers. It hadn't completely penetrated. Not until now. She wasn't fooling around with school-yard bullies. These were trained killers.

This wasn't some foolish adventure where she could dodge successfully ten steps ahead of her hunters. The men she sought to elude had found her twice, quickly. Had Lucas not been there… She would be dead. Possibly tortured first.

"Get my cell phone out of my pocket," Lucas instructed her. "Call nine-one-one. Get some officers out here fast."

This time she did as she was told without a second's hesitation.

LUCAS DISABLED THE BAD GUYS' car, which will get us out of this particular pickle. But they'll get another car. And they'll find us again. The question is how.

Those killers were on us almost as soon as we crossed the Mobile-Tensaw Delta area. They didn't recognize the rental when we passed them on that little county road. Or if they did, they knew the cops were hot on their trail, so they didn't try anything.

But they were at the condo in a matter of moments from the time Miss Shutterbug placed the call. Yes, even a bad guy could put it together that she'd found the cell phone in the condo. It was a likely possibility. But they'd sprayed the building with bullets, as if they knew where she was.

And now to turn up in this abandoned camp. As if there weren't thousands of miles of secluded areas in which she might have hidden.

And why are they trying to kill her? Lucas said they'd want to grab her and torture information out of her. Make her tell where Lorry might be. Because Lorry is the witness, the one person who can identify Antonio Maxim as the man who'd murdered Harry West.

We're back out on the county road. I hope the humanoids realize that lunchtime has come and gone. Out here in the country, where folks work hard each day, the three regulars need a bit of supplementation. An afternoon snack and then a bit of bedtime sustenance.

One of the few bad things about my job is that whenever I'm on a case, I lose weight. Clotilde likes a tomcat she can wrap her paws around. None of that sleek, alley-cat charm for her. Well-fed, well-groomed and well-loved. That's the ticket that turns my Clotilde on.

Let's see if I can convince these two that we need a food break as soon as we get close to some sort of civilization. I hate to say it, but even a fast-food burger would taste delish now.

"YOU CAN TAKE THE CUFFS off."

Lucas almost swerved off the road as he

glanced at Michelle. She actually sounded contrite. And judging by her expression—the tinge of pink in her cheeks and the willingness to meet his gaze completely—she was sincere. "Fool me once, shame on you. Fool me twice... I'm sure you know the old Scottish saying."

"I do. And I won't. I realize that I'm wrong. I've been acting like an idiot."

Lucas glanced at her again. It was difficult to judge the depth of her remorse. The winding road that went through deep forests and then patches of clear-cut, bald land with startling curves and steep drops took all his attention. For a Texas man who'd considered Alabama to be a Gulf Coast state, he found the land to have a surprising degree of roll.

"And I should believe you?" he asked.

"Yes."

"Give me one good reason."

"Because I want to help Lorry. So far, I've only made it impossible for you to help her. I see that now. Those men will kill me or anyone else who gets in their way. I'm a danger to everyone I come in contact with."

Had she really grasped the enormity of the danger she faced? He wanted to believe her. Strange how much that was true.

He'd forced the image of her coming out of

the lake from his mind. He'd caught her unaware, and it had made him feel like a Peeping Tom, so he'd tried to eradicate it from his mind. But he couldn't. If Michelle would actually work with him, there were ways she could help.

"I want to believe what you're saying." He left it at that.

"I can't undo what I've done. God knows I would if I could. Everything I did, though, was an attempt to make things right."

He nodded. "I do believe that part."

"Okay." She shifted in her seat so that her handcuffed wrist rested an inch from his leg. "Now I understand that the best way I can help is to do what you say."

"Just that fast?"

"I've been shot at twice. Those men managed to find me in the most out-of-the-way place on earth." She shrugged. "I have to say I'm outclassed. I don't know the rules of this engagement. Worst of all, I suspect there aren't any rules."

She was bright, that much was evident. "Hold the wheel," he told her. They'd hit a straightaway, and she could steer from the passenger seat. He fished the handcuff key from his pocket and gave it to her.

She unhooked herself, returning both key and cuffs to him.

"What are we going to do?" she asked.

"Call Marco at the gallery. He's worried sick about you. And your parents."

Dismay flickered briefly across her face. She'd rather face the Maxims than call her folks. That said a lot.

He passed her his cell phone, and she took it and dialed.

"Hello, Marco. It's—" She stopped, her expression shifting to stricken. "No." Tears slid down her cheeks.

"What is it?" Lucas asked. He slowed and looked for a place to pull over.

"Are you sure?" Michelle asked.

Lucas couldn't hear the answer, but when Michelle lowered the phone, he took it from her hand.

"Marco, it's Lucas West here. What's going on?"

"Kevin Long seems to be missing. He failed to show up for a job, and he hasn't spoken with any of his friends since last night."

"Do you think someone abducted him?"

"Kevin isn't the kind of man who misses a photo shoot. Not one for *Vanity Fair*."

"Who saw him last?"

"He was at a restaurant, having dinner with

friends. They all left together. Kevin got into a cab, and no one has seen him since. I went to his apartment. I don't think he made it home last night."

"Has anyone reported him missing?"

"Not yet. Tell me what to do. Should I call the police?" Marco asked.

"Don't call anyone." Lucas was playing with Kevin's life. A wrong decision…

"Why not?" Marco asked.

"I don't trust the feds, and I'm not sure who I can trust in the NYPD. Let me handle it. I'll make sure they're looking for Kevin."

"How is Michelle handling this? Does she understand how serious this is?"

"I don't know." She was already beating herself to pieces about her involvement with Lorry's situation. Kevin was a direct link to her. She'd never forgive herself if anything happened to her friend.

And she'd never forgive him if his decision not to call in the FBI cost Kevin's life. He was trying to balance the protection of Lorry, Michelle, and now Kevin.

Funny how the first woman he'd felt this kind of visceral attraction to seemed destined to be taken from him. He sighed. "Keep me posted if you hear anything from Kevin. Right now we've got to find a safe place."

"Can I do anything to help?" Marco asked.

"Call her parents, and tell them she's okay. And then take a vacation. Go somewhere no one would ever think to look."

"Good advice."

"If you hear anything, call back at this number."

"Will do."

Lucas hung up and found a dirt road that looked unused. He turned down it. Michelle sat stone-faced in the passenger seat. She looked neither right nor left, and one lone tear hung on her cheek.

When he stopped the SUV, he brushed the tear away. "This isn't your fault."

"Right."

"It isn't, Michelle."

"Then whose fault is it?"

"The Maxim brothers. You stumbled into this. You didn't ask for any of it to happen."

"Neither did Lorry. All she did was the right thing by testifying."

"That's true."

"And now I've ruined her new life, and my friend has been abducted by gangsters who will torture him because he's my friend." Her voice broke, but she managed to hold back the sobs.

Lucas put a hand on her shoulder, and

without further encouragement, she turned into his chest and began to sob. He held her, gently stroked her arm and back and let her cry it out. When the storm of emotion had passed, she eased away from him.

"I'm sorry." She defiantly brushed the tears from her eyes. "I'm not normally a crybaby."

"I don't think you're a baby at all," Lucas said, and he meant it. He pushed a strand of her beautiful red hair back from her eyes. "You've been pulled into a lifestyle of violence and cruelty. You didn't deserve this, Michelle. And you're right. Neither did Lorry. But I want you to understand I'm here by choice. And we'll figure out a way to find Kevin. My brother still has some friends in the NYPD. I'll make some calls."

"Would you?"

He nodded. "But we have to move out of this area. The Maxims have found us once."

"Won't they be in jail? We called the deputies and nine-one-one."

"I'm sure they had another car somewhere close. They were likely picked up and on the move by the time we were ten miles down the road."

"How many of them are there?" she asked.

"If I were an apocalyptic kind of guy, I'd say legions." He smiled to show her he was gently teasing.

To his utter surprise, she leaned across the console and kissed his cheek. "Thank you. I know you're trying to make this easier for me."

Lucas merely nodded. Now he was the one bearing the cross of guilt. Her friend was held captive by ruthless thugs, and he'd given her hope that Kevin might be okay. His was a deliberate act of deception.

Chapter Twelve

As Lucas drove across the long span of bridge over the Mobile-Tensaw Delta waterway, Michelle composed herself. The only other time she'd fallen apart had involved her parents and their attempts to thwart her career plans. And that was a place she didn't want to go.

Guilt, shame, self-doubt—all of those things she was familiar with. She'd been well-trained by well-meaning people who truly wanted her to achieve her "full potential." She didn't fault her parents, but she'd learned how quickly they could erode her budding self-confidence and belief in herself.

The news about Kevin had triggered all the self-doubt she'd worked so hard to leave behind.

Lucas was kind to tell her she wasn't responsible, but none of this would ever have happened if she'd given him the negatives and memory card from Lorry's wedding. If she'd done that one thing, she'd be in New York now, celebrating her photography exhibit and sipping champagne with Kevin and Marco. Her life would have advanced toward the goals she'd so carefully chosen and worked so hard to attain.

The black cat seemed to sense her thoughts. He leaped from the backseat into the front and crawled into her lap. The wind whistled through the broken windows of the car, and she wasn't surprised when Lucas pulled into the first big service station.

Dozens of cars were lined up in the park-and-ride beside the station. It wasn't until Lucas cruised the area that she realized what he intended to do.

"You can't steal a car," she said.

"I'm actually very good at it."

"I don't mean you physically can't. I mean it's wrong."

He gave her a look. "We can't drive around in this vehicle. In case you haven't noticed, the air-conditioning system comes from a series of bullet holes."

She caught the laugh in her throat and then let it out. She'd never have believed the man could make her laugh, especially not about such a dire situation. "Why can't we just rent another car?" she asked.

"Because the first car I rented is back at that camp. This is the second one. I don't think the rental agency is going to be happy to see this car. It's a little the worse for wear."

He had a point, but he was also a law officer. Well, he once had been. "Couldn't someone make a few calls on your behalf?"

He hesitated. "I'm not sure I can trust anyone."

What he didn't say spoke volumes. Michelle felt the chill travel up her spine. If Lucas didn't trust other law-enforcement agencies to help him, where did that leave them? "I wonder how Maxim's thugs found me," she said.

He stopped beside a Volvo and appraised it. "Yeah, I'm wondering the same thing. I can't afford any more chances or mistakes. We're lucky to be alive. Or at least I am. If it wasn't for Familiar warning us, I'd be dead, and you'd be wishing you were."

"Why are they trying to kill me?" Michelle asked. "You said they want to capture me and force me to tell where Lorry is."

"They aren't trying to kill you."

Michelle knew her face showed incredulity. "Automatic-weapon fire. Twice. Car destroyed, condo sprayed with bullets."

Lucas parked two rows down from the Volvo and shut off the engine. He turned to her.

"Make no mistake about it. If Robert had given the word to kill you, you would be dead. This is all a game to him, Michelle. He thinks he's in the catbird seat, and he's having fun."

"Fun? That's insane!" She was outraged.

Lucas smiled and shook his head. "My point exactly. The Maxim brothers are insane. They're savage and ruthless, and they take pleasure in the suffering of others. What sane person could ruin the lives of innocent young girls?"

She didn't have an answer; it was just another step in her reeducation. The world was not all a place of art lovers who grew misty-eyed at the sight of a photograph of the Hudson River landscape or one that captured two little girls in a state of total bliss as they played together.

That was her world, but it wasn't a place where the Maxims lived.

"Why is Robert Maxim so arrogant that he feels he can play with us like this?" She had to know. What kind of man defied the law so openly—to the point of killing a law officer?

"Right now we can assume that Robert has Kevin, and he expects that will bring you to heel. He'll call in a bit and tell you. He'll make you decide whether Kevin lives or dies."

She could see how hard it was for him to

tell her, but he was preparing her. "I don't know anything." She spoke softly, but it sounded like a plea.

"I know that."

"How can I make him believe me?"

"I don't think you can."

"Because I told him I knew." She turned her face away and struggled to compose herself.

"You did *what?*" Lucas asked, as if he hadn't clearly understood her.

"I used a cell phone I found at the condo and called him and told him I knew."

He fought not to show his dismay, but she saw it. "I brought this on Kevin, didn't I?" she asked.

Lucas had gained control of himself. "Robert would have been looking for some leverage no matter what you did or didn't do. Because of the wedding photograph, he believes you know Lorry or something about her. He didn't need encouragement to jump on this. I told you that at the beginning."

She swallowed the lump rising in her throat. On top of everything else, she wasn't going to be a crybaby. She eased the phone from her purse and started to punch in the numbers.

"What are you doing?" Lucas asked.

"I'm going to call Robert and tell him I'll give him what he wants if he lets Kev go."

Out of nowhere the cat's paw reached up and snatched the phone from her hand, flinging it into Lucas's lap. He grabbed it and slammed it shut.

"What is wrong with you?" Michelle fumed. "Give me back that phone."

"Not on your life." Lucas examined it. "This could be how they followed you."

"The phone?"

"It's possible that the Maxims have sophisticated tracking devices and systems installed. Highly possible." He popped the back of the phone open and removed the battery. A tiny chip rested in the corner of the battery compartment. Lucas fished it out and tossed it through one of the blown-out windows of the SUV.

"Is that it?" Michelle leaned forward, ready to grab the phone. As soon as she got a chance, she'd call Robert. She'd trade herself for Kevin. He was totally innocent, and she was to blame for all this.

"I never got into technology, but—" He hit the On button and checked the phone. "It works fine without that chip, so I'd say that might have been a GPS plant."

"Now what are we going to do?" she asked.

"You and Familiar get out and walk toward the truck stop. I'll hot-wire the car and pick you up. Just act natural, and when I stop, get in quickly."

She nodded. There was no point in arguing now. Lucas was in charge.

Just as she opened the door to get out, the phone Lucas still held began to ring. He checked the caller ID, hesitated, then handed it to her.

She noted the Dallas area code. "Hello."

"Have you made up your mind to cooperate?" the male voice asked.

"I'll do what you say." She sounded tired and defeated even to her own ear.

"Where are you?" he asked.

She hesitated while Lucas grabbed a notepad and pencil and wrote *On the way back to Mobile.*

"I'm heading back to Mobile now."

"Someone will meet you at Felix's Fish Camp on the causeway."

"What time?" she asked.

"At six. Dump the marshal, and tell him for me, he's going to join his brother underground. It's just a matter of time."

Michelle was spitting mad. "You sorry sack of—"

Lucas grabbed the phone from her and snapped it shut. "Don't provoke him."

"He said he was going to kill you."

Lucas nodded. His gaze was on the truck stop, where a busload of middle-aged women was unloading for a rest break. "I've become a thorn in his flesh." He arched an eyebrow at her. "And I intend to become a stiletto in his heart."

"It's just that he assumes he'll kill you and get away with it, like it was nothing." She bit her lip. "He's going to kill Kevin, isn't he?"

"Unless we figure out a way to stop it. The problem is, Kevin is in New York, and we're down here." He put a hand on her arm and gave it a gentle squeeze. "But Harry still has friends on the NYPD force. As soon as we get a different car and get moving, I'll call some of them and put them on it. I'll trust them as much as I can."

"I'm supposed to be at a restaurant on the causeway at six this evening. Do you think Robert Maxim will be there himself?"

Lucas rolled his shoulders. "Robert is an arrogant man. He likes to handle things personally. Antonio had the same trait, which is why he personally shot Harry. He could have sent a hired gun, but he wanted to do it himself. There's a good possibility Robert will show tonight. And this may be our only chance to find out where he's holding Kevin. Now, I want you to do exactly what I tell you."

His instructions were interrupted by the ringing of his cell phone. The number wasn't familiar, but he answered quickly.

"Lucas, it's me. I'm okay. Don't hunt for me."

Michelle sat forward at the expression on Lucas's face.

"What?" she asked.

Lucas spoke into the phone. "Lorry, the appeal has been—" He closed the phone.

"Is she okay?" Michelle asked.

"She is. For the moment. I didn't get a chance to tell her the appeal had been pushed up."

"What are you going to do?"

"Get us down the road."

LUCAS WASN'T KIDDING when he said he could hot-wire a car. He boosted this Volvo in the park-and-ride in a matter of seconds. He's a careful man. He needs to be. The more I've heard about these Maxim brothers, the bigger I see the trouble Michelle and Lorry are in.

The good news is that Lucas got a message from Lorry. She said she was okay. That was it. No indication of where she was, but Lucas will track her when it's safe. He isn't going to risk Lorry's life. And he had no doubt she was using a disposable cell phone. He's taught her all the tricks to keep herself out of harm's way.

As it is, I'm watching over the sleeping Miss Shutterbug. Lucas gallantly stole a vehicle that allows the seats to fold down and create a snuggly rest area.

Lucas left me with explicit instructions to alert him if Michelle wakes up and tries to go anywhere. He's making a few phone calls himself, and I don't think he wants her to hear the gist of his calls. Something has to be done to help Lorry and Kevin.

Whoever would have thought that by attending a simple wedding in Spanish Fort, Alabama, I would end up in the middle of a Texas-mob adventure?

Life for a sleek black detective is one exciting moment after another. The bipeds should take note. Like my humanoid counterpart, the intrepid 007, I am always well-dressed, always urbane, with never a hair out of place.

Ah, the princess stirs. Let's just hope she reads Lucas's note that tells her to stay put and that she abides by his command. I'm ready for some chow, and if Miss Shutterbug misbehaves, that will only delay mealtime.

"I'D APPRECIATE ANYTHING you can do," Lucas said softly. "I'll be glad to wait until Will Bennett can talk to me."

He stood looking at the gently lapping water of Mobile Bay. To the south, above the water, the Jubilee Parkway spanned the breadth of the bay and delta area. The Mobile Bay Causeway, a man-made strip of narrow land, was the original roadway across the bay.

He'd learned that the area was once a thriving tourist zone, where fishermen came to catch the crabs and flounder that proliferated in the brackish waters.

Though over a hundred miles from the landfall site of Hurricane Katrina, the causeway was almost destroyed by the tidal surge that swept along the Gulf Coast from Louisiana to Florida.

While many of the hotels, restaurants and service stations had not rebuilt, the natural environment of marsh grasses and water birds was coming back. He watched a huge brown pelican coast over the water. It was a beautiful area. A place where he imagined life was serene and bountiful.

From his vantage point, he could see both the city of Mobile and the bluffs of Spanish Fort on the eastern shore of the bay. Not fifty yards away, parked in the shade of several willow trees, was the vehicle where Michelle napped, Familiar at the ready. He had to smile. The cat was everything Eleanor had said he was. Never again would he doubt her word about the animal's amazing abilities.

A voice came through the phone. "Lucas, it's Will Bennett here. We did a thorough check, very discreetly, as you asked. Kevin Long is missing. He hasn't shown up for work. No one has filed a missing person's report yet, but it won't be long. His friends and family are beginning to get concerned."

Lucas had held out a tiny hope that Robert Maxim was bluffing—that he hadn't snatched Kevin. Now that hope was gone. Kevin Long *was* missing, and no one who knew him or worked with him could account for his whereabouts.

Which meant that Robert had him.

And would kill him.

"Will, do you have anyone on the inside of Maxim's New York business?"

There was silence. "I can't discuss that. You turned in your badge." There was a long pause. "Maybe you should pin the badge back on."

"Maybe." It wasn't the first time Lucas had thought about it. He needed the authority of the law and the right to carry and use a weapon if he was going to protect Michelle and keep Lorry safe. But being a free agent also had benefits. He was no longer bound by conduct that would prevent him from doing whatever was necessary to protect the two women and see Antonio Maxim rot in prison.

"Why are you so interested in Kevin Long?" Will asked.

Lucas hesitated. He'd grown distrustful of everyone. Even his fellow marshals. Somewhere, deep in his heart, was the fear that one of his fellow officers had betrayed Harry. How else had Antonio known exactly where to find his brother? How had the criminal known the exact location? Yet Will had been Harry's close friend. Lucas had to make a choice—either he could trust Will or not. And he dang sure needed someone he could trust.

"The witness in the appeal against Antonio Maxim has been compromised."

"Holy—" Will broke off.

"I know. Anyway, the witness is on the run, and I have reason to believe she's safe enough. For the moment. But the problem is that Kevin Long is an associate of the photographer who accidentally blew the cover on the witness."

"So Robert Maxim has snatched her friend to try and force information out of her."

"That's pretty much it in a nutshell."

"And you guys are where?"

"South Alabama."

"I won't even ask why. I'm sure that's a mystery you'll never be able to explain."

Lucas couldn't help but smile. Will, a third-generation New York police detective, had never seen the beauty of the South, or he wouldn't have to ask why. "I need someone to find out where Kevin is being held."

"Easier said than done, my friend. While Robert Maxim is down in Texas, his organization is still highly effective up here. And since Antonio was arrested, they've gotten more clever about hiding their activities."

"Before he was shot, Harry told me that he and his partner had infiltrated the Maxim interests in New York." Lucas put it on the line. Either Will would help or not. "Could you ask his partner?"

"I'll see what I can do. No promises."

"I understand. But if you do turn up something, will you call me?"

"What can you do down there without legal authority?" Will asked.

"The fact that I'm not in law enforcement may be an asset."

"Hey, we don't need any cowboys going for shade-tree justice."

"Will, my brother is dead. I'll take justice pretty much any way I can get it. Just let me know if you find Kevin."

"You either get your badge back or go home to your cattle ranch and stay out of this." Will's voice was stern. "You pop a cap in Robert Maxim, you'll be charged with murder. You know that, Lucas. For your brother's sake, don't throw your life away."

"Thanks, Will." There was a lot of truth in what the NYPD officer said, but Lucas knew he wasn't ready to listen to it. At least not yet.

He put the phone in his pocket and headed toward the vehicle. He wanted to prep Michelle for her meeting tonight. Robert was more reckless than his older brother. If he showed up in person—a gesture meant to let Lucas know how powerless he was—Michelle might be able to turn it to their advantage.

Lucas had a few tricks up his sleeve. One required a stop at an electronics shop.

Chapter Thirteen

Michelle kept her gaze focused on the restroom wall of the Charco-Burger fast-food diner. Lucas's warm fingers traced the flesh of her chest and torso as he taped the wire into place. He was the ultimate professional, but that didn't keep her from blushing. The wire ran between her breasts, and as he secured the microphone and wire, he was explaining how the device worked.

"I'll be able to hear everything that happens," he said. "I'll also make a tape."

"That's good." She couldn't help the nervous flutter in her voice.

"Michelle, you can do this without blinking an eye, but understand that you don't have to. I won't kid you. This is dangerous. If Robert actually shows up in person and he suspects you're wired—"

"Right. I know what will happen. If he

doesn't kill me on the spot, he'll certainly kill Kevin." At last Lucas was finished, and she tucked her shirttail back into her jeans.

Along with the equipment Lucas had purchased, she'd gotten new clothes and a blouse made of thick oxford cloth in a dark green. It was the best she could find to cover up the wire.

"Now, what is your objective?"

"To get him to tell me where Kevin is." That was her main objective.

"And what else?" Lucas prompted.

"To get him to talk about anything criminal. Murder, attempted murder, extortion, whatever."

"Robert likes to brag. If we can get anything criminal from him on tape, we can pick him up and force him to tell us about Kevin."

"If I screw this up, Kevin will die." She said it softly.

Lucas put a hand on her shoulder. "It's possible Kevin is already dead."

She turned away and washed her hands at the bathroom sink. There was a loud knock on the door.

"Let's get out of here," Lucas said.

"People are going to talk." She tried to interject a light note as he unlocked the door and they both walked past a startled woman with a toddler in tow.

"Hey, this is a woman's bathroom," the woman called after them. "Damn perverts!"

Michelle felt the color heat her face, but she didn't turn around. Lucas had already picked up some burgers—an entrée that Familiar was not pleased about. He was a hardworking cat, but he had definite palate issues. High class. High maintenance. Once Kevin and Lorry were safe, she'd see that Familiar had a seafood smorgasbord that would put five pounds on his sleek frame.

She settled into the front seat, and Familiar hopped into her lap. He head-butted her chin a few times and kneaded her thigh, purring loudly.

Lucas got behind the wheel and drove slowly down the steep bluff to the causeway. They'd already scoped out the restaurant where she would meet Robert or his emissary. Lucas had found a place where he could watch a large part of the restaurant through the huge window that fronted the bay.

When he pulled into the parking lot, she had five minutes.

She took a deep breath and started to open the door. To her complete surprise, Lucas caught her hand and pulled her toward him. The kiss he gave her was passionate and fast. For one brief moment, she forgot about the danger and the Maxim brothers and allowed herself the luxury of the white-hot desire that flooded through her.

When he broke the kiss, she was breathless.

"Be careful," he said.

"I'll do my best." She felt flushed and unsettled.

"I didn't want you to go up there without knowing that I care about you. And I have every confidence in you."

She felt a lump in her throat. "That means a lot to me, Lucas. More than you know."

"String him along. Let him think you know where Lorry is, but that you won't give a shred of info until Kevin is released."

She nodded.

"Robert won't try to hurt you in public. But he will try to scare you."

"I understand." They'd been over this before, but she knew this was how professional law officers prepared. Repetition, repetition, repetition. It might save her life, or Kevin's.

"I'll be over there in the marsh grass, with the binoculars. Try to manipulate him to a table with a view."

"Will do." Impulsively, she leaned toward him and placed a gentle kiss on his lips. "I didn't want to leave without letting you know how *I* feel."

She was smiling when she ducked out of the vehicle. As she hurried toward the ramps that led up to the door of the restaurant, she didn't notice the small black shadow that darted behind her.

As she slipped through the front door, Familiar was at her side.

LUCAS CHECKED THE EQUIPMENT for the hundredth time. He could hear only a roar and a clatter, until Michelle spoke. He had her clearly, the tape recorder whirling. As soon as he was certain the conversation would be taped, he got out and moved to the blind afforded by the tall marsh grass. He had a perfect view of the restaurant window, and just as he'd hoped, he saw Robert Maxim hold Michelle's chair for her at a table right beside the huge window.

Like it was a date.

The idea made him bunch his fists, with an eager desire to connect with Robert's handsome face. Yet again, Lucas realized he simply didn't understand the dark drives of Antonio and Robert. They were both handsome men, well-educated, cultured, who'd inherited an empire from their father.

It wasn't need or desperation that had sent them into the white slavery business. It was greed and a desire to inflict pain and suffering on those weaker than them. To him, the Maxims were the worst of what evolution had brought about in humankind—strong, intelligent men who sought to destroy weaker individuals. And Lucas intended to take them out, any way he could.

"I'm not very hungry," Michelle said in response to Robert's question about whether she wanted an appetizer.

"The lady will have the crab claws and a glass of champagne."

"The lady is not interested in alcohol or food." Michelle spoke calmly, but her tone was an affront to Robert. Through the binoculars, Lucas could almost see Robert's face harden. *Good for Michelle.* She was playing it perfectly.

"Bring the food and champagne," Robert said. "Now."

The waiter hurried away, and Robert leaned toward Michelle.

"Where is Betty Sewell? Or shall I call her Lorry Kennedy?" Robert said.

"Where is Kevin?"

"You aren't in a position to bargain." Robert sipped his water.

"Release Kevin, and I'll tell you what I know."

"How am I to be sure you know something worthwhile?"

"You abducted my friend. You must think I know something of value."

Robert chuckled. "You're a clever girl, aren't you?" The waiter brought the champagne and poured two glasses. Platters of food arrived.

From his position in the marsh grass, Lucas could only watch, helpless to assist Michelle. But she was handling it fine. She had grit and courage and attitude.

"First of all, I'm not a girl, Mr. Maxim. I'm a grown woman. And I have a question for you. Why are you here in person? Why not send one of your hired hands for this?"

Lucas wanted to hug Michelle. She was perfect. She was taking the offensive, which Robert would never expect.

"I like to tie up loose ends myself," Robert said, tension in his voice. "And I heard you were beautiful as well as talented. I have a need for a photographer. Some of the young ladies who come to me need portfolios. For their modeling careers, you know."

Michelle didn't respond, but Lucas could almost sense the answer she wanted to give, which would have been explicit and rude.

"Take it easy," Lucas coached her, though she couldn't hear him. "Don't let him provoke you. That's his game. He wants to see if he can shake something loose."

"I didn't realize meth addiction required models," Michelle said, with a smile. "Imagine the bone structure I could capture on film."

"I don't find your insults amusing, Ms. Sieck. I have no idea why you'd link my name with meth addiction."

"Oh, I guess I wanted to hold off with the white slavery charges until later in the evening. Once we got cozy."

"Would you like to speak to your friend?" Robert asked. His tone was hard.

"Yes."

Robert brought out a phone, dialed, and held it out to Michelle. She took it and raised it to her ear.

Lucas could hear only Michelle's response, and he caught the sob in her throat as she said, "Kev, are you okay? Where are you?"

Robert reached across the table and took the phone. "I'm negotiating with Ms. Sieck. If I don't call you back in fifteen minutes, do what must be done."

"You kidnapped him, and you'll kill him, won't you?" Michelle asked.

"Indeed," Robert said. "Now I'm tired of your games. You come here thinking you can provoke me without consequence. That's the action of a very foolish woman. Then again, women are mentally inferior. But that topic bores me. Where is Betty Sewell?"

It was all Lucas needed. He had the conversation on tape. It was enough to put Robert behind bars. But first, Michelle had to get out of there.

"I have to know that Kevin is free. You can kill him at any moment."

"Don't make me angry," Robert said. "You spoke with him. He's uninjured. For the moment. Now tell me what I want to know."

Michelle leaned forward. "The witness is in Austin, Texas. She's in a safe house."

"The address." Robert's voice was sharp, eager.

"I don't have it, but I can get it. Lucas can find out. I just need some time to get it from him."

Robert drained his champagne. "You have until tomorrow morning."

Michelle pushed back her chair. "I'll get the information, but I won't tell you until Kevin is free."

"And how will you convince West to cooperate with you?"

Michelle leaned closer. "That's not your problem, now, is it? I'll call you when I have the information."

Some sixth sense must have alerted Robert. He reached out and grabbed the front of Michelle's shirt.

Lucas came out of the marsh grass, his hand going instinctively to the place where his gun should be.

"Let me go." Michelle was completely unrattled. She grasped his hands and wrenched them free of her shirt, which had come partially unbuttoned.

"If you try to roll over on me, you'll regret it," Robert said.

Lucas could see that several people in the restaurant had stood up and were watching the confrontation.

Michelle leaned even closer. "Stick it in your ear, creep."

Robert suddenly let loose a howl of pain. He jumped up from the table and began to hop around. Several people started to laugh.

"Get out of there!" Lucas urgently whispered. Even though Lucas couldn't see, he knew exactly what had happened. Familiar had been under the table and had latched on to the mobster's leg with sharp claws and teeth.

"Get it off me!" Robert commanded as he jumped and bobbled.

Calmly, Michelle walked away. When she got to the door, she held it a moment for

Familiar to dart out. Behind her, the restaurant was in pandemonium.

"Lucas, 212-555-1212—that's the number he called when I spoke to Kevin," Michelle said into the hidden microphone as she went toward the car. Their plan was that she would drive away, alone, then circle back to the eastbound lane of the causeway, where he'd meet her.

She executed the plan perfectly. Whatever else Michelle Sieck might lack—like good judgment and patience—she was certainly long on courage and panache.

The black cat hopped into the open car door, and Michelle followed. Her red taillights were leaving the parking lot when Robert Maxim appeared at the doorway of the restaurant. He half shook a fist.

Lucas knew that Michelle had hooked him well and thoroughly. He wouldn't harm Kevin until he had the information he thought Michelle could give him. That put her in more danger than ever before, but it would buy some time for her friend. And as soon as Lucas was certain Kevin was unharmed and free, he'd turn the tape over to the law-enforcement agencies involved. But not until he was positive both Lorry and Kevin were safe.

Lucas dialed Will Bennett at NYPD and

gave him a rundown on what had just happened. He also gave him the phone number Michelle had recited.

"It's a cell phone," Will said, "but we can run a location on the call. Good work, Lucas. With any luck, I can have a SWAT team there in under twenty minutes."

"Be careful. Robert's men will kill the hostage. And I'll pass your compliments along to the woman who deserves them."

He hung up and dashed through the tall grass and across the four lanes of the causeway. According to their plan, Michelle turned on her right-turn signal before she began to slow.

When she drew abreast of him, Lucas jumped in the car before it had time to coast to a stop. "Just keep driving," he told her. "I think we're in the clear, but I don't want to take any chances. And turn around at the first chance. We need to get back. If we can track Robert, we may get the jump on him in more ways than one."

As he spoke, Lucas scooped Familiar into his arms. "Did you see this guy?"

"Oh, did I ever." Michelle reached across and scratched the cat's ears. "He was stupendous. You have no idea. He was hanging on the back of Robert Maxim's butt like a Tasmanian devil." She started laughing.

Lucas joined her. The relief flooding his body told him how tense he'd been. How much he cared about what happened to Michelle.

"And just to show that I'm not totally ungrateful…" Michelle handed Lucas her purse. "Dump it, please."

He did what she asked, immediately catching the smell of the delicious fried seafood. He looked at Michelle. "You didn't!"

"Oh, yes, I did. While Robert was dancing around, I scooped up the crab claws for Familiar. I knew he was dying from lack of good seafood, and I didn't want them to go to waste."

Lucas leaned across the seat and kissed her on the cheek. "If you ever went into a life of crime, you'd be extremely dangerous. Lady, you have—"

"Fortitude," she supplied.

As she eased the car over beside a Dumpster, where they had a good view of Robert getting into his big Lincoln Town Car, the laughter died.

"Want me to drive?" Lucas asked.

She considered it. "I can manage."

He leaned back, Familiar in his arms. "Good. I need a session of affection with the big guy here. And I thought my blue heeler was smart."

"Never underestimate a feline," Michelle said. "Or a female."

"That lesson is well and truly learned," Lucas said, pulling out the binoculars and reading off the license plate of Robert's car so Michelle could write it down.

MICHELLE IS THE BOMB. Not only did she stand up to that creep, Robert Maxim, but she snatched his crab claws and brought them home to Daddy. And I have to say, light, crisp crab claws, with a hint of garlic and lemon— these are delicacies from the abundance of the Alabama coast. This might truly be God's country, at least for a seafood-loving cat.

All in all, a rather good evening. Michelle got a lead on Kevin Long's location; Lucas got a tape of Robert Maxim confessing to kidnapping and threatening to murder, and I got a hunk of Robert's muscular ole but-tocks. That's one biped that will be standing for the next several days.

I'd love to know what's running through his mind, other than fantasies of harming Michelle. The man is seriously angry at women, and Michelle intentionally pushed the edge of his envelope. He's not going to forget or forgive.

She outsmarted him, outmaneuvered him and outright challenged him. Now he's going to try to make her pay. Which was the scheme all along. When Michelle first drugged Lucas and headed out on her own, she was determined to be the bait to draw the Maxims after her instead of Lorry. Now I think she's succeeded beyond her wildest dreams. Robert is going to come after her, and he's going to enjoy hurting her—if he gets a chance.

But that's where Cowboy Lucas and I come in. We'll protect Miss Shutterbug. And hopefully, we'll snare Robert in his own trap. That would give me ultimate pleasure. Even more than clawing and chomping on his derriere.

We're headed across the causeway, back to Spanish Fort. There's a wonderful old hotel in Point Clear, and I'll bet you my bottom dollar that's where Robert is holing up. Perfect. The place couldn't be better designed for a takedown. Some of the rooms are isolated, with plenty of space for a SWAT team to maneuver. Once Kevin is located, Robert is going down.

Chapter Fourteen

The adrenaline rush had begun to recede, and while Michelle drove with the ease of a New Yorker, she could feel the tremors of nerves tingling through her thighs. Jelly legs. If she tried to walk right now, she might drop to her knees.

She'd confronted Robert Maxim, and she hadn't backed down, just as Lucas had coached her. The strategy they'd chosen to employ involved bravado and bluff. Now that it was over, she realized how truly frightened she'd been. Thank goodness for Familiar. Otherwise, Robert Maxim might have tried something at the restaurant.

The problem was that even focusing on the late-evening traffic along Scenic Highway 98, she couldn't push the image of Robert's dark, malevolent eyes out of her mind.

She tailed him into a charming town. Fairhope.

So aptly named. Lush flowers adorned every street corner, and twinkle lights were strung in the Bradford pears along the streets.

Robert continued through the town, and for a moment, as they headed down a steep hill, she wondered if he was going to the water. Perhaps he had a boat—which would greatly complicate the plan Lucas had mapped out.

Instead, he took a left and headed along the shore. Michelle kept well back without Lucas having to warn her. Traffic was almost non-existent, and she kept plenty of road between the two cars.

Fifteen minutes later, he pulled into a hotel with a guarded gate. She glanced at Lucas.

"Keep going," Lucas instructed her. "The man has some audacity. He sits in a restaurant and threatens you, then heads to a fancy hotel."

"Shouldn't we call the local authorities?" Michelle asked.

"We can't, unless we're willing to risk Kevin's life. I have someone working on it in New York."

"So we wait?"

"That's exactly what we do."

She pulled into a small service station and turned around. "There's a neighborhood across from the hotel. We can park there and watch."

"That's the good thing about a hotel with

one entrance and a guard post. We can keep up with who goes in and out." Lucas tried to sound upbeat, but she could tell he was exhausted.

She found the road and drove in, killing the lights on the vehicle. The night was brightly lit, and she found a parking spot in the protection of a beautiful mimosa tree with a clear view of the hotel entrance.

"Why don't you try to rest? I'll watch," she offered.

The black cat put a paw on her mouth.

"I think Familiar is telling you that he'll take the first shift," Lucas said. "He is danged amazing. When this is over, I'm taking Familiar and Eleanor out for the finest meal D.C. has to offer."

"Me-ow!" Familiar agreed.

"Let's get some shut-eye. We might not have another chance." Lucas slid down in the seat and tilted his head back.

Michelle did the same, but she was too keyed up to sleep. She glanced at Lucas. For a moment she thought he'd already given in to exhaustion, but he turned to her, his gray eyes clear in the light that filtered into the car from a nearly full moon.

"I'm too tired to sleep," he said.

"Same here." She hesitated. "Would you mind telling me about your brother?"

When he didn't answer immediately, she

started to apologize. He picked up her hand and held it, gently stroking the fingers.

"Harry was a great guy. We grew up on a ranch out in West Texas. It was a lot of hard work, always cattle to find and doctor and round up. Miles and miles of fence to ride and repair. By the time we were both ten, we were working alongside my dad and the other hands."

"That's a lot of pressure for a kid," she said.

"In some ways, yes. But in others, we had the best childhood possible. Sure, we worked, but we also played baseball in the summer and touch football in the winter. Heck, we were driving the farm trucks before we could see over the steering wheel. We'd stand up and drive. My dad taught us responsibility, but he didn't stint on the praise."

The image he drew was so different from anything she'd ever known. "Tell me more," she said.

"Harry was my best friend. He taught me things. He looked out for me. He was the good guy that everyone looked up to in high school. Athletic, competent, honorable. He married Janice right out of high school."

"Did that upset your folks?" she asked.

"Are you kidding? Janice was the catch of the century. She adored Harry. And when he decided to go into law enforcement, she agreed to leave the life she loved on the ranch and move to Dallas. It was a big sacrifice, but that's the way their marriage was. They both put the other first."

"I always wished I'd had a sister," Michelle said. "Someone to help shoulder the burden of disapproval from my parents."

"Maybe if you'd had a sibling, they wouldn't have expected so much of you." He hesitated. "I spoke to them, Michelle. When I couldn't find you, I called and warned them. I urged them to go to a safe place."

"I'm sure they went ballistic, wondering what I'd done now to make such a mess of their lives."

"For some people, being critical is all they know."

"That's a fine explanation if you aren't the one who is always being criticized."

The pressure of his fingers increased on her hand. She never talked about this to anyone. She didn't want Lucas to think she went around feeling sorry for herself because she didn't have adoring parents. "I've done okay with it. I followed my dream, and I learned to live without their approval."

"I don't think parents understand how important approval is," he said. He brought her hand up and kissed it lightly. "From my perspective, though, you're one helluva woman."

Her first inclination was to throw up an emotional barricade. Praise always came with a price, from her experience. But her hand felt so warm and protected in Lucas's grip. And he had nothing to gain by saying what he'd said. She took a deep breath. "Why did Harry become a Dallas police officer?"

"He always had that sense of right and wrong, and when he decided to go into law enforcement, the Dallas PD was hiring with a fast promotion track. He felt he could best support Janice and the family he wanted by joining the force."

"And you became a marshal?"

Lucas laughed. "Now that was a more romantic choice. Just the image appealed to me. And I preferred the Austin area. Still not as big a city and lots of land nearby if I had a yen to ride my horse."

"Are your folks still on the ranch?"

"You bet. They're a tough couple. Dad still works the cattle, and Mom cooks and feeds the twenty farmhands. Heck, if Dad quit paying them wages, they'd stay for Mom's cooking."

"I'd like to meet them one day."

"When this is over, I'll take you there. I

bought a place north of Austin, more toward the center of the state. But we'll drive over to Mom and Dad's. I think they'd get a charge out of you. Heck, you'd be a big-city celebrity in Limestone County, Texas."

Talking with Lucas was like falling off a log. She began telling him things she'd never expressed to anyone. Not even Kevin.

At the thought of her friend, a prisoner who was possibly being harmed, the tension returned to her body.

"What's wrong?" Lucas asked.

"Kevin."

"We're doing everything we can. In fact—" he punched the stem of his watch so that it glowed in the dark "—I should hear from Will before too much longer."

Lucas had told her about Bennett and the SWAT team, but she was too afraid to even hope. If they could free Kevin, then she and Lucas could call in backup to arrest Robert in his hotel room.

Visualizing the look on Robert Maxim's face as someone snapped cuffs on him made her intensely happy. "Do you think Kevin is still alive?"

Lucas nodded. "No reason for Maxim to kill him. Yet."

"And Lorry?"

"As far as I know, she's safe. Robert wouldn't be talking to you if he had Lorry. She's a smart gal. She didn't leave a trace of trail behind her."

"I disrupted her entire life."

"It wasn't deliberate, Michelle. You've got to learn to forgive yourself for honest mistakes."

"Now that's easier said than done."

For a moment they were quiet. Lucas continued to hold her hand, his thumb making gentle circles. It was such a pleasurable sensation. A week ago, if someone had told her she'd be sitting in South Alabama with a former U.S. marshal, keeping watch on a Texas mobster, she would have scoffed.

"If we succeed in getting Robert Maxim arrested and charged with kidnapping and attempted murder, what happens next?" she asked.

"That would be the best possible outcome. With Robert behind bars, I think the Dallas and New York PDs could break the back of the Maxim organization."

"And Lorry could live a safe life?"

"Yep. And you, too."

"Then that's what we have to do."

"I like your determination. Now try to rest. I'm going to do the same."

Lucas lifted her hand for one more kiss.

Then he held it against his chest as he leaned back and closed his eyes. To her surprise, Michelle discovered that the talk had relaxed her, too. She slumped down and closed her eyes. She didn't even remember falling asleep.

AREN'T THEY CUTE? *A couple of Sleeping Beauties. And a good thing. All that chitter-chatter was distracting me from my job as lookout. I gotta say, standing guard in a vehicle is a lot different than lounging against a saddle at a campfire. I've done a little of that, too. At least here in this affluent area of South Alabama, there aren't wolves or bears or coyotes. There are some mighty big snakes, though, and one slithering around the area is Robert Maxim. I just don't buy the fact that Robert took a public humiliation and slinked off to his hotel room.*

Funny, but at first glance, I thought he was a handsome man. Of the tall, dark and virile variety. Expensive clothes, well-groomed. Easy to see he came from money. A man with his physical grace and looks could have gone anywhere. And then I looked into his face and saw that he had the eyes of a dead man. There's not much that money, makeup, or even plastic surgery can do for a man whose soul is dead.

I've worked some tough cases, but Robert

Maxim is a breed of criminal that I haven't seen a lot of, thank goodness. Greed, desperation—those are things that I don't like, but I can at least comprehend.

Robert, and apparently his brother, Antonio, had the world at their fingertips. They had money and a plush lifestyle. Their father was a respected businessman who is likely turning in his grave at what his sons became. What thing twisted the two boys into such monsters? That's a question that's a bit too big for even Familiar, the black cat detective. All I know is that neither brother can be allowed to remain free.

Eleanor told me a bit about Harry West's death. Harry had followed the trail of two young girls who'd been lured up to New York City by the promise of a glamorous life as a model or a TV star. They'd left their small Texas towns and headed up to the Big Apple on a bus. There, someone from the Maxim organization had met them. Before they could say "photo shoot," they were working the streets to pay for the bus ticket and cheap room in a sleazy hotel. To make sure they stayed in line, the Maxims introduced them to meth. Euphoria for ten seconds and then a lifetime of suffering. And a short lifetime at that.

Harry did a lot of legwork, with the help of

the NYPD. He found the girls and spirited them out of the Maxims' network. Once they were in a rehab center and cleaned up, they agreed to testify against the Maxims.

The case was almost closed, and Harry was going to be the prime witness against Antonio. Then he got a call from one of the girls. She was in trouble. He called for backup but went on ahead. Antonio Maxim was waiting for him. Harry came around a corner, and Antonio stepped out of a car and shot him point-blank in the heart and the head. He died within seconds.

Antonio got in his car and drove away. The two girls, Ellie and Ginger, were also found dead. Someone had shot them in the hotel room where they were supposed to be safe. There were phone calls from the hotel room to Antonio Maxim, which indicated that the girls had lost their nerve or couldn't handle the craving for more drugs and decided to return to the Maxim stable. There was also a call from one of them to Harry's cell phone, which must have been the distress call that he rushed to answer.

Complicated scenario. Especially when it's crossed my fevered little brain that perhaps someone was sitting in that hotel room with Ellie and Ginger, with a gun pointed at them to make one of them place that call.

Call me an untrusting feline or a paranoid feline or a clever feline. Doesn't really matter. I have my instincts, and I trust them. Which is why I'm sitting guard right this minute. Something tells me that Robert Maxim heading to his hotel room like a whipped dog doesn't ring true. He's up to something, and I intend to be sitting right here when he or his minions show up to try to hurt Miss Shutterbug and Cowboy Lucas.

It's almost midnight now. The moon is bright and clear, and I spy movement near the guard post at the hotel. The guard is a courtesy, a service of the hotel to protect guests and visitors from intruders who might be looking to break into cars or rooms.

There's no reason for the guard to pay attention to a guest walking out empty-handed. Or what appears to be empty-handed. I know better. This guy is armed. All very well-timed, too.

Let me awaken Cowboy and his sleeping photographer. I think they need to be ready for this.

Chapter Fifteen

Michelle awoke to a cat paw on her lips and the not-so-gentle head-butt of Familiar, forcing her out of slumber.

"What?" She sat up.

Lucas put a hand on her shoulder. "Start the car, but don't turn on the lights."

She didn't waste time asking questions. Lucas's voice let her know this was serious. She glanced across the road to see if Robert Maxim was on the move, but the driveway into the hotel was empty.

Which meant that someone on foot was out there.

At last she caught sight of a dark shadow moving along the palm trees beside the high brick wall of the subdivision in which they'd parked.

"Get us out of here," Lucas said. "Head east."

She punched the accelerator and roared out onto the road, squealing the tires as she turned left. Expecting gunfire, she was surprised when the guy in the shadows merely ducked behind a tree.

She was half a mile down the road before she turned on her headlights. Lucas was kneeling in his seat, watching behind them. Familiar was right beside him.

The dashboard clock showed they'd been asleep for only half an hour. Which meant they'd been had by Maxim from the get-go.

"Why didn't he shoot?" she asked as they continued.

"That troubles me," Lucas admitted.

Before he could say anything else, his phone rang.

"It's Will."

She felt the tension in him. "Can you put it on speaker?"

"Sure." He answered the phone, and she could hear the New York accent of Will Bennett.

"We found the place they were holding Kevin Long, but they moved him," Will said. "Sorry, Lucas. We got there quickly, but he was gone. We spent a while searching the area, hoping to find some leads. The place was cleaned by a professional."

"Nothing?" Lucas's voice held disappointment.

"Nada," Will said. "These guys are thorough. There wasn't even a gum wrapper or cigarette butt."

"Turn around."

Michelle didn't realize he was talking to her until he touched her shoulder. "Turn around. Quick."

The road was empty, as if all around her had settled in for a long sleep. Michelle executed a U-turn in the middle of the road.

"Why are we turning around?" she asked.

"Will, you've got to get a lead on Kevin Long."

"It isn't as if we aren't trying." Will sounded defensive.

"I know that. But we're in a delicate place with Robert down here. We can't keep this stalling game going for long."

"I have some news, and I suspect you aren't going to like it." Will said. "Antonio's appeal is definitely set for Thursday. The prosecutor couldn't get a delay."

Michelle could see the stricken look on Lucas's face. His tone indicated the depth of his shock. "This has to be postponed, Will. There's no way to produce the witness that fast."

Bennett's voice was loud enough for her to hear. "The marshals surely have a handle on her, right?"

"Will, she's missing. No one has located her." Lucas exhaled, and Michelle could see the struggle it took to keep his voice steady. "If Maxim is pushing for an early court date, they know we can't produce Lorry."

"Either that or they're counting on the fact that she's too afraid to show up in court. Damn it, if she doesn't show, he'll walk. If Antonio wins the appeal, he can't be tried again for Harry's murder."

"Antonio is smart. He's making this situation work for him." The muscle in Lucas's jaw flexed.

"I guess they figured you could flush her out of hiding."

Lucas's features froze into an expression of fury. When he spoke at last, his voice was neutral. "Who expedited this appeal?"

"Judge Franklin ruled, and that was it."

"Exactly how is the witness supposed to know the appeal date has been changed?" Lucas's voice now held an element of danger.

"I don't know. I'm just a city cop, and I don't talk to the marshals about witnesses or to judges about court dates. The only thing I can come up with is that everyone thinks you have her stashed, Lucas."

"This is a death sentence for Kevin Long, Will. I can't believe this has happened. It's clear to me that the judge doesn't want the witness in the courtroom."

"What can I do?" Will asked.

Michelle began to slow the vehicle. They were close to the hotel. She scanned both sides of the road, looking for an ambush, hoping Lucas would tell her what he had in mind.

"Get the prosecutor to get a delay."

"How?"

"Be creative, Will. You have to postpone this appeal until I can find Lorry and get her to New York. You have to find a way."

"Lucas, you sound way too much like Harry now. He took matters into his own hands, and it got him killed."

"Antonio Maxim will pay for my brother's murder, and I'm taking Robert down with him. Enough is enough, Will. If the justice system is going to work to aid and abet these criminals, then I'll do what I have to."

"You're talking dangerous stuff." Will's voice came through the phone sharp and upset.

"Then don't listen." Lucas snapped the phone shut and held it so hard that Michelle thought he might crush it.

"We're at the hotel." She had slowed to a crawl. There was no evidence that anyone was about. She wanted to talk to him, to say something that would reassure him, but she didn't know what to say. She reached across and touched his arm. "I'm sorry."

"Go down the road two miles, and turn around again."

Though she wanted to argue, she didn't. Kevin's and Lorry's lives were at risk, and Lucas had already lost his brother. There wasn't anything she could say that would change this.

Without Lorry's testimony, a murderer would go free.

Now wasn't the time to point out to Lucas all the things that could go wrong. Whatever it took, she would help him.

"Me-ow." Familiar nudged her elbow with his head.

And Familiar would help, too.

As they approached the hotel entrance for the fourth time, Lucas reached out to touch Michelle's arm. She'd been a strong, silent support as he'd tried to come up with a way to find Lorry and get her to New York and save Kevin Long. There was really only one course of action open to him. It wasn't a good choice. In fact, it was a downright bad one. But he didn't see any other way.

"Michelle, I'm getting out by the marina. I want you to keep driving around this area. If I'm not back in half an hour, I want you to head north. Seriously north. Like Idaho or Minnesota."

"Because you'll be dead?"

"There's a chance of that. And if Lorry doesn't testify, then Antonio will be cut loose. He'll do everything he can to extract revenge on anyone he thinks worked against him."

"So I'll lose everything."

"I'm sorry. I wish you weren't involved."

"If I weren't involved, we wouldn't be in this situation." She held up a hand. "Broken record, I know."

"Promise me that you'll leave in half an hour."

"Sure." She put a hand on his arm and squeezed. "If I'd done what you told me from the first, maybe things would be different. You're the expert. But if you need to find me, I'll be—"

"Don't say it." He covered her mouth with his hand. "Don't tell me anything that could put you in danger."

"You're afraid they'll torture you." Her voice broke as she said the words. "Lucas, I can't just drive off and leave you."

"You have to. I'm counting on you." He

could see the tears in her eyes, and he swallowed hard. "If I know you're safe, I'll be okay."

"Surely we can think of another way, another plan where you don't go in there alone. He has at least three men with him. They're armed. We should go buy a gun or something."

"We don't have time."

She grasped his hand and kissed the palm. "I don't know if I'm strong enough to do this," she said.

"You are." He nodded. "Stop here."

She braked, and the car rolled to a stop. "Lucas…"

He leaned toward her and kissed her. He couldn't help himself. Why hadn't he found this woman years ago, back when Harry was alive and his world was a place of hope, with the promise of a future filled with love and family?

Her response made his body clench. Michelle didn't hold back. Not in her photography or her courage or her passion. Her lips were soft and hot and demanding, and for one long moment, he forgot everything except her.

It was only headlights approaching from behind that made him break the kiss. If he could have stayed in that moment for the rest of the night, it would have been bliss. But too much was at stake.

"You gave me your word. Half an hour, then leave. Get a different car. Pay cash. Then get out of here."

"I promise."

He touched a silvery tear as the car passed them, highlighting for one moment the sadness in Michelle's eyes.

Before he could weaken, he opened the door and stepped into the darkness. High shrubbery gave him the cover he needed. If Robert Maxim wanted a war, Lucas would take it right to his door.

WHAT IS WITH MISS SHUTTERBUG? She dried her tears on the back of her hand. Punched the gas and took off like a, well, a scalded cat. Isn't that the most vulgar expression you've ever heard? Repulsive, actually.

If one is to use slang, I much prefer the dog references— crazy as a run-over dog. Now that's descriptive. And how about this one: as happy as a one-eyed dog on a gut wagon? Lovely Mississippi colloquial descriptive term.

Let me see, an expression to indicate haste. How about as frantic as a humanoid at a going-out-of-business sale? Yes, I like that much, much better.

But to the point. Miss Shutterbug has zoomed down the road to a service station. She's filling the car and also filling a small gas can. And now she's inside, paying and buying a cigarette lighter. But she doesn't smoke, and I don't think we're going to build any campfires.

So what's up?

Uh-oh, she's driving back toward the hotel. I can see that she must have had her fingers and toes crossed when she gave Lucas her word that she would leave. The truth is, I never expected she would. That concession was far too easy. A few tears, a flame-seared kiss. He was putty in her hands.

Men. They just never learn. As if Michelle would suddenly turn into a tractable, docile, obedient feminoid. Right. And that's exactly why I adore her. She's exactly like a feline. Independent, stubborn, and determined to be in on the action.

Let 'er rip, Michelle. I'm with you all the way.

THE SECURITY GUARD WAS young and bored. Michelle sized him up in a matter of seconds as she pulled up beside the booth where he sat with a sports magazine in his hand.

"Hello," she said.

"Can I help you, ma'am?" he asked.

"Depends, Officer." She smiled. "I need to find the front desk. I'm here for a photo shoot for *Prime Resort* magazine, and I'm running very late."

"Straight down the road. Pull under the portico, and you can check in there. They'll help you find your room."

"Thank you, sir." She gave him another smile. It never hurt to be charming; that was one lesson she'd learned from her parents that served her well.

She felt the cat's gold-green gaze on her, and she reached out to scratch his head. "It's part of the game, Familiar. Don't act so shocked. You do it all the time, rubbing against people and pretending to be so cuddly." She found the spot on his back that drove him wild and gave it a gentle scratch. "I'm learning from a pro."

She pulled under the portico and held the door for him as she entered. "I'll distract the clerk at the desk. You find Robert Maxim's room."

The cat scooted across the lobby before anyone noticed him. He disappeared at the desk. There was a big advantage to being short, black and sleek.

"Hi. I need to check in. Pamela Anderson." It was the first name she could think of.

The clerk, a young woman with sharp green eyes, gave her a long look but began the process of looking up her name.

"I'm sorry, but there's not a room reserved here for you."

"But there must be." Michelle could play confused. It wasn't far from the true state of her mind. "I booked it weeks ago. Full spa treatment, room with a view of the water. It's my present to myself for the divorce."

The clerk returned to her keyboard, tapping in her name again. "Ma'am, I am sorry. I don't have a thing."

Michelle willed the tears to form in her eyes. She let them slide down her cheeks. "This isn't possible. This is the only thing that's kept me sane. Bobby got the house and the kids and the horses. I'm left with nothing. This was to be my last fling."

The clerk hid her annoyance pretty well. "Come over here and sit down," she said. "Let me get you a tissue."

By the time she'd stepped into the office, Familiar was at the keyboard. He was gone before the clerk returned.

"Here you go," she said to Michelle, offering the box of tissues. "Let me see what we can do. Maybe there was a cancellation."

"It's okay." Michelle stood up. She took a

tissue and wiped her cheeks. "It isn't the end of the world. I can drive on to the beach and find something there. Thanks for your time."

She all but ran out of the lobby, leaving the clerk looking at her as if she'd lost her mind.

Chapter Sixteen

Lucas used his knowledge of Robert Maxim's ego to narrow the room choices. Robert's accommodations would be the most expensive, most well-appointed in the hotel. A ten-dollar tip to a waiter making room-service deliveries confirmed where Robert was staying.

One thing about Robert's superior attitude, it made everyone willing to rat him out. Robert had been needlessly rude to the waiter; therefore, the waiter had remembered him and been delighted to give up his room number.

Lucas approached the bungalow, which fronted a sweeping lawn shaded by magnificent live oaks draped in Spanish moss. With the moonlight filtering through the tree limbs, it was a scene from a black-and-white movie of an elegant era long past. Beyond the lawn, the bay whispered against the shore in a seductive promise. With the beautiful moon and the stars, it was paradise.

Taking a deep breath, Lucas allowed himself one fantasy of Michelle. If only they could share this view together, standing outside the door of a bungalow, then walk inside, close the door and shut away the danger and desperation in their lives. Shut away all the negative things and meet as a man and a woman with an electric attraction between them.

He could see her red hair spread across the white pillow of a bed. She was a beautiful woman, from the top of her head to her toes. And she was a fighter, a woman with spirit. While she knew nothing of ranch life, she reminded him of the strong women who'd made his early life such a joy. If she chose to, she'd easily confront the challenges of the ranching life. She'd confront them and prevail, because Michelle was that rare combination of fire and strength.

Michelle's kiss had been a heady rush of heat, desire, electricity and need. If the kiss was any indication, she would be every bit as hot as her hair color indicated.

He shook off the fantasy and approached the bungalow carefully. Before anything else, Robert Maxim had to be neutralized. Then Lorry would come out of hiding and testify, and then, if the photographer gave him half a chance, he'd find out what really made her tick. What an adventure that would be.

The draperies were drawn across the window, and he couldn't hear a thing inside the bungalow. He would count on the element of surprise—because that's all he had. He didn't even have a weapon. Somehow, he'd have to get a gun from one of Robert's henchmen. That would be tricky, but he could manage it. He'd find one of the men working security, surprise him, neutralize him and take his weapon.

"Psssst!"

He froze.

"West!"

He turned slowly, expecting to find a gun pointed at his heart. Instead, he saw a shadowy figure in the azalea bushes that grew thick and dense beside the hotel.

"Who are you?" Lucas asked.

"A friend."

Lucas didn't exactly buy that answer. "How so?"

"Get away from the door before they open it. Come over here. Now!"

Lucas hesitated, but he moved toward the shrubs. He didn't have a choice. If this was one of Maxim's security men, he would shoot

Lucas in the back if he tried to run. A more likely plan was to get Lucas deeper into the shadows and then attack with a knife or garrote. Something silent that would leave Lucas dead.

"Who are you?" Lucas asked again. He kept his body casual, but he was tensed for action.

"I'm a friend of your brother's. Harry and I were working the Maxims."

Lucas wasn't certain he'd heard correctly. "A friend of Harry's? You're NYPD undercover?"

"That's past tense. There was a disagreement on how to proceed, so I left the job. I was undercover on the Maxim case when Harry showed up in New York. We were about to close the door on Antonio's fingers when Harry was killed."

"What are you doing down here?" Lucas asked. An outdoor light cast dim illumination around the exterior of the hotel, but it was good enough to see the fortyish man with sandy-gray hair and an imposing build. Despite the dim illumination, Lucas could tell the guy was in top physical shape. He braced for an attack.

"The same thing you are. I'm here to take Robert Maxim out, one way or the other. Antonio is going to get the full ride for murdering Harry. If it means I have to kill Robert to keep him from interfering, then that's the way I'll play it."

"Are you—"

"Yeah, I'm part of Robert's security detail. I went undercover nearly two years ago." In the dim light, Lucas could clearly see the lines of tension in the man's face. "When Harry was killed, NYPD tried to pull me back in. I broke contact with the force, and I held on with Robert, hoping and waiting for the right time."

The man was a rogue cop. Much like Lucas. That was the thing about the Maxims—they pushed good people over the line.

"I tried to make contact earlier tonight," the man said. "I was with Robert at the restaurant and knew you were tailing him. I got out at the gate and saw you park at the subdivision entrance."

Lucas recalled the figure that had approached the car when they were parked in the subdivision. "When we were in the car?"

"Yeah, but you took off. I wanted to try to coordinate with you about Robert. We've got to do something and fast. He's got a hostage in New York, and he'll kill him. I've heard him talking about this guy. He's a friend of your female buddy."

"Yeah, we know. The problem is, we don't

know how to help Kevin. And the courts have pushed up Antonio's appeal."

"When? And why?"

Lucas stared into the pale gaze of the man whose name he didn't know but whom he instinctively trusted. "They know Lorry is on the run. Antonio's defense team has worked the system. They figure if Lorry doesn't show up to testify at the appeal, then Antonio will walk out of there a free man."

"And he will—"

"If we don't stop it."

"That's right."

"You have me at a disadvantage. What's your name?" Lucas asked.

"Greg Lovett. Used to be Lieutenant Greg Lovett. I heard that you turned in your badge."

"I thought everything was set. Antonio's appeal would be over, and he'd be returned to prison for the rest of his life. I resigned so I could go to New York and watch the trial as a private citizen. I was done with law enforcement, anyway." Lucas shrugged. "Now I consider myself on special assignment."

Greg's eyebrows arched. "Do you have legal authority to arrest Robert?"

"I've got all the authority I need to take him down."

They shared a look, each reading the other.

They were both men who'd left law enforcement behind, both because of the brutal murder
of Harry West.

"I need a weapon," Lucas said. "When I hung
up my badge, I was planning to raise cattle and
mind my own business. This just got out of
hand."

Greg reached into his jacket. "That, my
friend, I can fix. The fact that neither of us has
legal authority could get a little sticky."

"I don't mind a bit of a mess as long as we
corral Robert and see that Antonio's conviction
isn't reversed."

Lucas stared at the solid door of the hotel
bungalow. "Listen, I have a plan. If you can get
Robert to the door, do you think we can take
him?"

"As in take him hostage?" Greg asked.

"Something like that. Hold him for ques-
tioning. We'll figure out a way to describe it
that avoids the term *kidnapping*. Look, we're
off the official ledger, so we can do whatever
we need to do. Robert may complain about it,
but I doubt a lot of people will listen."

Greg's smile was wide, his teeth glinting in
the dim light. "I like the way you think. In fact,
it reminds me a lot of Harry."

"Folks always said we were like two peas in
a pod."

"I can see that. You even look like him. That's how I knew who you were when I saw you." Greg laughed. "When we came up on you two at the old camp in the woods, you looked exactly like Harry when he was surprised."

"You could have killed us, but you didn't."

Greg nodded. "Robert wants the woman alive. And I deliberately aimed high. Shattered some glass, made it dramatic."

"Thanks," Lucas said.

"Don't mention it. Now, once you get Robert, what do you intend to do with him? I mean, do you have a safe house to hold him in?"

That did present a small problem, since Lucas didn't even have a vehicle. "That's a bit of a quandary. I—"

He didn't get a chance to finish. He felt the brush of a small, warm body against his ankles.

"Me-ow."

"What the hell? It's a cat," Greg said, stepping back.

"Not just any cat," Lucas said, knowing that he would enjoy watching Greg come to accept how exceptional Familiar was. "This is Familiar, the black cat detective. He's on the case with me."

Greg looked at Lucas as if he'd lost his mind. "You're kidding, right?"

"Not a bit of it." Michelle's voice came from behind them. "You boys are slipping if a photographer can sneak up behind you."

"We were distracted by the cat," Greg said, a little flustered. "A black cat detective. Whoever heard of that?"

"You'll see that it's true," Lucas said. "I didn't believe it at first, but the cat is amazing. And now that he's here, along with Michelle—" he reached and caught her hand, pulling her against him "—I think we can make this happen."

"What's the plan?" Michelle asked.

"I've got to check in with Robert every twenty or thirty minutes," Greg said. "Fill her in. I'll be back in about ten." He stood up and walked to the front door. At a triple knock, the door opened and he stepped inside.

"Who is he?" Michelle asked.

Lucas explained, bringing her up to date on what he'd learned.

"And you're going to abduct Robert Maxim?" Michelle asked. There was worry in her tone.

"*We're* going to abduct him."

"Are you forgetting that he has weapons and we don't?" Michelle asked.

Lucas held out the automatic Greg had given him. "We don't have the same firepower, but we are armed. Once we get our hands on Robert, they won't shoot for fear of hitting him."

"And this will help how?"

He could tell Michelle had a lot of doubts about the plan, and he didn't blame her. It was an act of desperation. But if he wanted to save Kevin Long and delay Antonio's appeal until Lorry could get to New York to testify, then he was going to have to take a risk.

"Once we have Robert, we can force Antonio to postpone his appeal, and we can make Robert's men let Kevin go."

"Like with a videotape of us torturing him?" Michelle asked.

"We can't really torture—"

He didn't finish, because she punched him in the arm. "I know we can't really torture him, but I can manipulate the film to show anything we want. You forget, before I became your partner in kidnapping, I was a professional photographer."

"How could I ever forget that?" Lucas asked. He felt a flutter of excitement. With Michelle's skills and Greg's help, they now stood a chance. It was a long shot, and one with plenty of risks, but it was the best chance he'd had since Lorry Kennedy disappeared.

OKAY, THIS IS SHAPING UP just fine. Greg is a great addition to this motley crew. And he's got the secret knock down pat. I can't wait for another tête-à-tête with Robert Maxim. Lucas says we can't torture him for real, but I do believe he's due for a bit of kitty-cat claw sharpening. Just a few digs in the back of his thighs to help me keep my razor-sharp little toenails in manicured condition.

Think of the meals I've missed—and the sleep—because of him. It's enough to make a black cat turn gray. And he's taken hostages and tried to kill us—he will kill Kevin and Lorry if he gets a chance. So I figure a little bit of torture might be good for him. And because I'm a black cat, I'm not bound by the conventions of the humanoids.

I'm a free agent, a roving feline 007. And James Bondocat would never shirk from a bit of necessary roughness. I'm not talking water boarding here, just a few sharp claw pricks in strategic places.

Okay, Greg is back, and he's making a routine perimeter check. Then it's showtime. I have to say, the sooner this is over with, the better I'll feel. I can get back to D.C. and my beautiful Clotilde. Back to the buffet of delicacies that Eleanor keeps on hand for me. I'm going to have to learn to take only cases where the people are dedicated cat lovers. I mean, Lucas and Michelle try, but my goodness, they don't understand the importance of fresh mahi-

mahi or perhaps a tender bit of liver. Hamburgers and dry cat food are not sufficient to keep my large, very active brain functioning properly.

But enough about food. Here we go. Get your pistols ready, Cowboy Lucas. We're headed to the O.K. Corral.

MICHELLE BROUGHT THE CAR around and opened the back hatch. She poured the gasoline around the doorway and returned to the car to wait. If all went as they'd planned, soon Robert Maxim would be in the back, with Greg holding a gun on him, and Lucas would be sitting in the passenger seat beside her.

Familiar was the backup. The cat could subdue Robert far better than a bullet. He had his ways.

She'd kept a careful watch for the regular hotel security, but the night was quiet. She'd seen only one young couple, obviously newlyweds, kissing under the beautiful oaks.

Now this was a place for a honeymoon, she thought. It was a place of history and beauty, and the fact that Lucas was only a few yards away made her heart beat faster.

Though she was vigilant and alert, she allowed her thoughts to wander to the ex-marshal turned cowboy. They'd gotten off to a rocky start, what with her catastrophic mistake with the wedding photograph. Lucas, though, had seen the truth. He knew she would never put someone in harm's way for her own personal glory. He'd seen that, and other things, and he'd been free with his praise.

That was such a remarkable experience. Each tiny compliment that he paid her was like salve on an old wound. Funny, because Marco and Kevin were always building her up. For some reason, though, Lucas's praise meant much more. Perhaps because they'd started at such a negative place.

And good lord, she could barely think of his lips without feeling a flush run all through her body. To prove the point, she shifted behind the steering wheel. If they ever got to a place in time when they weren't on the run or on the offensive against killers, she wondered if they would act on the red-hot desire that was always there between them. The fantasy images that popped into her head made her fidget in the seat. Lucas was that rare combination of strong and sensual. He paid attention to the reactions of others, and she knew that was the key to a fabulous lover.

At thirty-two, she'd dated all kinds of men, but none gave her that high-voltage jolt of combined desire and respect that Lucas generated. He stood for something, and he didn't go around bragging about it. He simply did what he felt was right, like he had some inner compass that pointed him in the direction of honor.

That accounted for the respect part. But the desire... How to account for that? Her mother's standards—designer suits, corporate job, social skills—were false. So Michelle had begun to create her own. Lucas's tall, lean body and weathered face were more designed for a billboard depicting the cowboy life than any Manhattan club. But there was something in the way he held himself, in his ability to be tender yet masculine, to kiss her and allow her room to kiss him back. Those were things she'd never thought of before, until Lucas.

The clock on the dash told her that the moment for action was fast approaching. While the fantasy of Lucas beckoned her thoughts, she pushed it aside. They were a team, and each member had to be alert and ready.

She kept her gaze on the door of the bungalow, waiting for Greg to give the signal knock and the door to open. Lucas would push forward and force himself into the bungalow, and that's when it would get really dangerous—and that was something she couldn't afford to think about. She had her job to do, just like the rest of the crew. That was where she had to focus all her energy.

Lucas had told her that each element of the plan had to be executed perfectly. If she did her part with machine precision, everything would go smoothly.

Familiar edged to the door frame, pressing his small, sleek body against the wall. He was one special cat, and when this was over, she was going to document his life with photographs. He deserved to be on the cover of magazines across the nation.

Greg came around the shrubs. He checked where Lucas was still tucked away.

She had to keep her position. Lucas had never lied to her. She could only hope that this wasn't the first time. That everything would go just as Lucas and Greg had designed it.

Suddenly Greg was at the door. He knocked. The door slowly began to swing open.

Chapter Seventeen

Michelle had never considered that fear might have a taste, but the pounding of her heart and the bitter tang in the back of her throat came from abject fear. Not for herself, but for Lucas and Familiar and Greg.

As the bungalow door swung open, the danger of what they were attempting hit her like a runaway train.

"Everything is clear out here," Greg said in a loud voice to the men inside the bungalow. Greg had told them that Robert had two additional bodyguards in the bungalow and another security man working the perimeter of the hotel premises, which was a large territory. He came by on hourly checks.

She could clearly hear Greg's discussion with a voice she recognized as Robert Maxim's. Greg leaned in the door frame.

"It's a beautiful night out here. You should

take a look at the oak trees against the night sky."

"You're not paid to stargaze," Robert said harshly. "Keep your eye on your business."

"Yes, sir," Greg said, sounding suitably contrite.

The night was so quiet, Michelle could hear the gentle susurration of the water against the shore.

"You want some coffee?" someone in the bungalow asked.

"Sure." Greg was starting to step inside when Lucas exploded out of the shrubs. He pushed Greg aside, just as they'd planned, and rushed into the room, gun drawn. Familiar was right at his heels.

Michelle started the car and drove up on the grass to park about two feet from the doorway. She kept the motor going and the windows down, straining to hear everything that went on inside. Her view was limited, but she saw Robert go scuttling across the room, followed by Lucas.

Two gunshots sounded in the still night, and she felt tears gather in her eyes. She couldn't see what was happening; neither Lucas nor Greg was visible. She saw a streak of black dart across the doorway. Familiar was on the move. That heartened her. All wasn't lost as long as Familiar was there.

She was leaning forward for a better view when the door slammed with great force.

She was shut out.

LUCAS HAD EXPECTED THE gunfire. Robert Maxim's boys didn't carry weapons for effect. They meant to use them. But thanks to Familiar, he'd been able to raise the gun's barrel so that the shots went harmlessly into the ceiling.

The cops would surely be on the way any minute now. Kidnapping, even for the cause of justice, was illegal. So he and Greg had to snatch Robert and make a fast getaway.

He ducked a swing and did a quick spin, bringing his booted foot up to his attacker's temple. The man went down like a sack of rocks. Out cold. There was only one man left, plus Robert Maxim, who was frantically searching for a lost weapon on the floor.

"Yee-ooow!" Familiar leaped from the mantle onto the guard's head. His sharp claws dug trenches in the man's forehead, so that a curtain of blood destroyed his vision. Greg followed up with a one-two punch that doubled the guy over and sent him crashing to the floor, unconscious.

Lucas pulled his gun and walked directly to Robert Maxim, putting the barrel against his forehead. "Get up," he said. The urge to pull the trigger, to put an end to Robert and his evil, was strong. The desire to avenge Harry's brutal death was even stronger.

"Lucas," Greg said softly. "Don't do it, man. Killing him is something you'll never walk away from. Harry would kick your butt."

Lucas gathered his reason and tapped Robert lightly on the head with the barrel of the gun. "Get up before I shoot you on the spot."

"I have no intention of going anywhere with you. You're an ex-lawman, and you have no authority to make me do a single thing." Robert looked at Greg with hatred. "You'll pay for this, you Judas."

"Not nearly as much as you and your brother will pay," Greg said. "Harry West was my friend. Your brother walked up to him on a sidewalk and put a bullet in his heart and brain. Antonio is going to prison for the rest of his life, and so are you."

"Dream on," Robert said. He was shaken, but he hadn't lost his bravado entirely. "One snap of my fingers and the hostage dies. And just so you know, *Mr.* West, we're on Betty Sewell's trail." He made a great show of looking at his expensive watch. "In fact, she might be my guest by now."

Lucas felt a rush of blood to his head. He

drew back his fist, intending to bash Robert's smug face to pieces. Before he could strike, he felt the sharp claws of the cat in his shin.

"Me-o-o-ow." Familiar shook his head from side to side.

"Is that cat telling you not to hit him?" Greg was so amazed that he bent down to stroke the cat's fur.

"He is," Lucas said, reluctantly lowering his fist. Nothing would give him more satisfaction than knocking a few of Robert's pearly whites down his throat. But Familiar was right. Now was not the time.

"For the last time, get up," he ordered Robert.

The mobster only smiled.

Familiar walked up to him, jumped into his lap and dug his claws into the tender flesh of his lower abdomen.

"Hey, I'll wring your neck!" Robert jumped up and lunged at the cat, but not fast enough. Familiar was at the door, and Lucas and Greg each had one of Robert's arms. Together they propelled him across the room, out the door and directly into the open hatch of the car.

He didn't even get a chance to protest before Lucas slammed the hatch, struck a match and tossed it into the gas-soaked grass and jumped into the passenger seat. Greg and Familiar tumbled into the backseat as Michelle spun out on the lawn. The tires finally grabbed, and the vehicle shot forward.

She took the winding driveway at high speed. When they passed the main lobby, Lucas could see that the gunshots and fire had created quite a stir. Hotel security, in force, was headed toward the bungalow, and in the distance, he could hear sirens. They were going to make a getaway, but just barely.

No telling what Robert Maxim's men would say to the police. If they were smart, they'd keep their mouths shut. They had Kevin as a hostage, but now Lucas held the trump card.

MICHELLE DROVE LIKE SHE'D never driven before. When the guard post came into view, she saw the security guy step out in front of the car. She hit the horn and never slowed. He leaped to safety only a second before she would have struck him.

"You guys are quite the team," Greg said from the backseat. "But as good as you are, I gotta say, the cat has more style."

"No kidding," Lucas agreed. "I told you Familiar was special."

"So special, I'm going to enjoy skinning him alive and then killing him." Robert Maxim had pulled himself into a sitting position in the cramped back quarters of the car.

"Ease up, Robert. You aren't in a place where your threats carry very much weight." Lucas didn't hide the displeasure in his voice.

"Where is my friend Kevin?" Michelle asked.

"I'm not such a fool that I'll tell you that." Robert lifted his chin, his arrogance returning even though his life was in danger.

"Oh, you'll tell us," Lucas said. "Familiar will see to that. And you'll tell us who's tailing Betty and where they are."

Robert gave the cat a hesitant glance. "You want me to believe the cat takes orders from you?" he asked.

"No one orders Familiar to do anything," Lucas said.

"Amen to that," Michelle agreed. "He does whatever he likes, and right now, I think he'd like to inflict pain. A lot of pain that can in no way be traced back to us."

Familiar didn't need another cue. He hopped onto the back of the seat and gazed into Robert's eyes. He lifted one black paw and placed it just beneath the mobster's right eye.

"That's some really tender skin," Lucas said. "Lots of nerves there. Also, the muscles of that skin play a role in vision."

"What's he going to do?" Robert asked. He was stock-still, as if he was afraid to move in either direction.

"Heck if I know," Lucas said. "He's his own boss."

"Get away from me," Robert said to the cat. He tried to dodge out from under Familiar's paw. The cat's response was to extend his claws and dig into the tender skin.

Robert yowled and froze. "Get him away from me."

"He'll leave you alone when he's ready," Lucas said. "Just keep in mind that he doesn't like people to be negative about his abilities."

"I don't know where you got this genetically deranged creature, but you won't—"

Michelle deliberately swerved the car so that Robert's head struck the window. "So sorry," she said. "You were just saying what about Familiar?"

To her total satisfaction, Robert chose to keep quiet. He turned away from all of them and looked out the back window, as if he hoped for rescue.

Michelle, too, kept a close watch in the rearview mirror. So far, there was no pursuit.

"You think they're looking for us?" Greg asked.

Lucas shook his head. "Robert's guys won't give up a thing. They won't tell the cops they were tricked by one of their own security men, not to mention a black cat and a woman." He grinned, and Michelle felt her hopes rise.

"How can you be sure they won't give us up as kidnappers?" Greg asked.

"Because they'll check on us. That's one thing we can count on. And when they do, they're going to discover that we aren't law enforcement any longer. We're rogues. And the most dangerous of any animals are rogues. We're capable of anything. They know we want to kill Robert, so to give us a good reason to do so would be totally foolish."

Robert snorted. "My men aren't fools. They'll be on your trail, and when they find you, you're going to suffer."

"Did you hear something?" Greg asked.

"Not a thing," Lucas answered.

"Me, either," Michelle said as she sped through the night toward the jewel of a town called Fairhope.

"Me-ow." Familiar put his paws on the back of the seat and gave Robert Maxim a long stare.

Silence filled the vehicle, and Michelle made the turn into the town. Spanish Fort and Lorry's house—which was perfectly empty—were their destination and not too far away. They needed a quiet, secluded place to do the job. With a bit of luck, they'd have Kevin free in no time, and if Robert wasn't lying about Lorry, then at least they'd have a lead on finding her.

But would they be fast enough to keep Antonio Maxim from reversing his jail sentence?

THE SUN CRESTED THE OAK trees, and Lucas ran through the video one last time. They'd been up all night, and Michelle had done a brilliant job of digitally manipulating the images into what appeared to be a sequence of severe torture inflicted on Robert Maxim. They'd used the computer in Larry's cottage and footage from a video camera they'd found in an all-night pawn shop.

The most impressive part of the entire video was that it never showed a blow landing or any other physical means of inflicting pain. The video was all clips of Robert screaming and begging for them to stop.

And it had all been done by Familiar. The cat had merely had to put his paw in a delicate spot and begin the process of extending his claws. Robert had screamed with gusto. Then Michelle had edited the film into what appeared to be a story of confinement and torture.

"This video is amazing," Lucas said to Michelle. There were dark circles under her eyes, and she looked exhausted. "You're a genius."

"I wouldn't go that far." She blushed and looked away. It was one of the things Lucas found so compelling about her. She was modest, and that was an old-fashioned and far underrated virtue in his book.

"I would," Greg said, patting her on the shoulder. "You *are* a genius. Where'd you learn to do all that with a cheap camera and some software equipment on a computer?"

She shrugged. "If I'd had my professional equipment, it would take a lab to detect the changes. As it stands, we can make this grainier, and it'll take them some time to find the ways we manipulated it. Hopefully, it'll convince them to release Kevin and tell us what they know about Lorry."

"The very best part is listening to Robert scream," Greg said. "Familiar was off camera, and he only had to threaten to claw him, and he squealed like a stuck pig. Very realistic!"

"Let's e-mail the clip to Antonio's lawyer." Lucas was ready to apply the pressure. Time was running out, and fast. They had little more than twenty-four hours before Antonio was due to appear in court for his appeal, and without Lorry there, he would walk.

He typed out the note: Postpone the

appeal, or Robert will suffer even more. Call us at this number when the appeal is postponed, and we will bargain with Robert's life. He'd included his cell phone number. Short, sweet, to the point. He loaded the brief video clip onto the computer and sent it off.

"If that doesn't stop them, nothing will," Greg said. "Now all we can do is wait."

"We have to find Lorry," Lucas said. He couldn't wait. It wasn't in his nature. If Antonio came up with some way to delay the appeal, it wouldn't be for long. The wheels had been set in motion, and no judge would postpone for any length of time. They'd bought an extra day, maybe two, at most. At the end of that time, the appeal would be heard, no matter what excuses Antonio could find.

"We have to find a way to get to Lorry and let her know that Robert has been neutralized." Lucas tapped his fingers beside the computer keyboard. "She'll return and testify if we can get word to her."

He looked over at the mobster, who was seething. He was tied in a chair. A mixture of red food coloring and corn syrup stained his white shirt. There were dark smudges on his face that looked like bruises; all had been artfully applied by Michelle.

"Antonio will recognize all of this for a fake," Robert said. "He won't fall for this."

"The icing on the cake, Robert, is that your own men will report to him that you were abducted at gunpoint by two rogue cops." Lucas smiled. "I have to say, this wasn't my original concept of how to fix this situation, but thanks to Michelle, Greg and Familiar, I think we've hit upon a pretty good solution."

"Antonio won't sacrifice himself for me." Robert almost growled the words. "Just as I wouldn't for him."

"He has no idea what you've told us, or where we may have deposited you. I'm sure Alabama will have some interesting charges against you. Attempted murder, for one. We could take you to the Baldwin County Sheriff's Office right now. By the time Texas extradites you, you'll be an old, old man."

Robert swallowed. "Your friend is going to die." He spoke to Michelle. "He will die a painful death because of you and these deeds."

Lucas saw the effect Robert's words had, and he went to Michelle and put his arm around her. She was courageous and smart. And so beautiful. "He's lying. All he's got left now is bluff. And if he keeps it up, we'll let Familiar play with him some more."

"Why don't you two grab some shut-eye for

an hour or so," Greg suggested. "I'm going to take a walk around the premises. Get the lay of the land in my mind. And Robert here won't be going anywhere. Your cat has already found a place to rest."

Familiar was, indeed, curled up on a plush sofa cushion in the sun. His work done, he'd already fallen into a deep sleep, his elegant black whiskers moving slightly as he breathed.

Lucas caught Michelle's eye. The idea of a couple of hours alone with her was like winning the lottery. They were tired, hungry and worried. Ever since he'd met her, they'd been in constant motion. Now, they could have some time to be still and be together, even if it was only to rest—although that certainly wouldn't be his first choice.

He saw that she was reading his thoughts. She blushed slightly, but she was smiling.

"Good idea," Lucas said. He stood up. "Call us if you need us." He made sure his cell phone was in his pocket and turned to loud.

Greg checked his watch. "I'll be right here. Robert, enjoy some time to meditate on your future. It looks pretty damn bleak."

Chapter Eighteen

Lorry's guest bedroom was beautifully decorated with the blues and greens that seemed so much a part of the lower Alabama landscape. Michelle turned to Lucas in the doorway. Now was the moment. She could feel her heart thudding. Somehow, in such a short time, their relationship had gone through a half dozen different stages. The problem was that she didn't know where she was in her own emotions. Things had happened so fast, and she didn't trust her feelings.

Dating in New York was so much easier. She'd meet an interesting guy. They'd e-mail and talk on the phone. Then a date would be set at a mutually agreed upon place—a restaurant or bar—where they'd dine or have a drink. Then they'd both take taxis back to their respective apartments.

Because they parted at the restaurant or

bar—unless other arrangements had been made—there wasn't a real opportunity for spontaneous intimacy.

Now, Lucas stood not six inches away. Her body and heart clearly knew what they wanted, but it was her brain that was sending warning alerts. In the past few days, Lucas had changed his view of her. He believed that the wedding photograph was an accident, and he'd come to respect her grit and courage. And there was a red-hot attraction between them that carried a jolt of pure sensuality. For the first time, though, Michelle realized that wasn't enough. She didn't want a few dates and a good time, or a fun and adventurous six months. Lucas was a man worth going the distance with, and she was beginning to realize that she was interested in a life partner. Something she'd never considered before.

"You did a great job, Michelle. If that video doesn't halt Antonio, nothing will." He cupped her cheek with his palm, and she marveled at how soft his touch could be when his skin was so calloused.

"Thank you." Her voice was almost a whisper. She cleared her throat. "We make a good team, Lucas. Me, you and Familiar."

"Yeah." His gaze shifted to her lips. She could sense the question he wanted to ask.

"My answer is yes," she said, shocked that the words had actually been spoken. She'd never been bold with men before, but she'd become much better, in recent days, at taking a risk.

"How did you know my question?" he asked, his hand sliding over her skin so that his palm caressed her jaw while his fingers stroked her neck.

"You wanted to know if you should kiss me."

"You must be psychic." He tilted his head and leaned down to meet her lips. His arms slipped around her waist, and he pulled her to him.

She moved her arms around his neck, glad to feel his strength and support because her knees had suddenly weakened.

Still kissing her, he stepped into the room and gently closed the door with his booted foot. "My goodness," he said, "I can't say I haven't thought about this, but I didn't think it would happen."

"Why not?" she asked. She could feel his heart beating against her chest, matching the quick pace of her own.

"We come from such different places, Michelle. You'll go back to New York, and I'll go back to my ranch. These will be stolen moments."

She pushed his dark hair back from his forehead. Suddenly, everything was clear to her. "The one thing I've learned since coming down here, Lucas, is that every minute is stolen. Something could happen to disrupt or destroy our lives even if we lived next door to each other and courted for ten years. I want to believe in a future, but I think we should take whatever joy life offers us. We should relish it and live it and not hold back. Because no matter how safe or perfect something looks, it can disappear."

His answer was another kiss. One that fueled the fire that was already burning. For the first time in her life, she gave herself totally to a kiss. She held nothing back.

Lucas picked her up and took her to the bed. He placed her gently upon it, never breaking the kiss. When he finally stood up, he looked down at her, the morning sun filtering through the gauzy draperies at the window. The muffled sound of birds could be heard through the glass.

"Woman, you may be more deadly than a Maxim bullet," he said as he slowly unbuttoned her blouse. He removed her clothes carefully, taking his time.

"I've run from real emotion all my life," she said. "Now I'm going to face it." Her smile matched her tone, and she saw that it aroused

Lucas even more. "Think you can handle it?" she asked, knowing that above all else, Lucas loved a challenge.

"I'm just about to prove that I can." Lucas unbuttoned his shirt and stepped out of his jeans.

I FEEL REFRESHED. A nice nap, and Greg found some cream in the refrigerator for me. In fact, he's scavenged up quite an omelet. Now all he has to do is get Miss Shutterbug and Ranger Rex untangled from the sheets and in the kitchen to eat.

I'm sure someone will feed Robert Maxim, but not for a while. He's too busy grumbling and threatening. He knows he's whipped, but he just won't accept it.

My keen hearing has been attuned to the sound of Lucas's telephone ringing, signaling a call from Antonio's lawyer. So far, nothing. I'd like to see them scrambling around, trying to come up with a reason to postpone an appeal that they fought so hard to set. It does my little kitty heart good to fantasize about such things.

It's strange. I was asleep for only a short time, but it's as if we've entered another chapter of this story. Felines are incredibly perceptive about time issues. Well, to be honest, we're just perceptive about everything. Like I can predict that when Lucas and Michelle come out of that bedroom, she'll blush, and he'll grin. There are just some things a cat can tell.

I feel much better after my nap, and even Greg, who got outside in the fresh air, seems to have recharged. Time hasn't really stopped, but we all needed an hour to recover from several long days of being on the run.

Since Greg is reluctant to disturb the love-birds, I'll do it. Hey, while I'm a fool for love, I'm also a practical detective.

Just a little nudge against the door. I hear them, awake and likely scrambling for clothes. My job is done. Oh, my, I wish I had time to call Eleanor and let her know somehow that Lucas has fallen under the spell of Michelle Sieck. When a six-foot Texan falls, he hits hard.

Now let's get some grub and pray the phone rings.

ALWAYS A MAN TO KEEP HIS personal feelings private, Lucas couldn't help the silly grin that he wore. No matter how much he tried to keep a straight face, one look at Michelle and he felt the muscles of his cheeks pulling tight and a goofy smile springing up.

Michelle, he noticed, was a fine pink where

a blush had stained her lovely white skin from her neck to the roots of her hair. And who said redheads couldn't wear pink! She looked incredible.

Lucas buttoned his shirt and glanced at Michelle as she did the same. Texas had its share of beautiful women, but none could compare with the fiery beauty that stood beside him.

"Once this is over, there's a conversation I want to have with you," Lucas said. He wanted to tell her about the ranch, about the day-to-day pace, where life took on the rhythm of a cattle herd, and about long, quiet nights filled with stars. Maybe it wouldn't be for her, but he'd never know if he didn't ask.

"Do you think this will ever be over?" she asked.

"We're close. Just hang on to your faith a little longer."

She turned to him, her hazel eyes searching his face. "You really believe that."

"I do."

The repeated bump against the door told him that Familiar was demanding to see them. He couldn't get upset with the cat. Heck, Familiar had saved his neck more than once.

"Let's see what's happening out there," he said.

Michelle followed him out the door. For one

moment, her fingers curled around his upper arm, and he felt a rush of pleasure. It was the signal that a woman used with her man.

He turned to her. The lines of tension were erased from her face. She was tired—they all were—but she looked like a...blushing bride.

"You guys hungry?" Greg asked. He waved a skillet filled with what looked like a Spanish omelet.

Lucas realized that he was ravenous. Michelle had filled an emptiness in his heart, but his body was demanding fuel, and the delicious smell of the sautéed onions in the omelet had his mouth watering.

"I'd love some eggs," he said.

"Me, too." Saying the words only deepened Michelle's blush.

Greg served the plates, including a share for Familiar. "I'll feed Robert last," Greg said. "Let him get used to the way it's going to be in prison."

"Have your fun," Robert said. "When I'm free—"

"Hell will be frozen over," Lucas interjected. "Just hope your brother's lawyer calls with the news we want to hear. But while we're waiting, we might have to have a little talk about Lorry, or Betty, if you prefer. If you really know where she is, you're going to tell us."

Robert glanced out the window, without a snappy comeback. Lucas registered the disappointment, but he kept eating. Robert Maxim had no idea where Lorry had gone. He was bluffing. Par for the course.

Lucas had just cleaned his plate and taken it to the kitchen sink when his cell phone rang. He checked his watch. Antonio's appeal would be heard in less than twenty-four hours.

"It's Benjamin Lumet here, Antonio Maxim's legal advisor."

Lucas looked at Greg and Michelle and gave them a thumbs-up. "Good to hear from you, Mr. Lumet. I hope you have the news we expect."

"The appeal has been delayed until Friday afternoon. I don't know what you hope to accomplish with this, but understand that I have lawyers in Houston working on filing kidnapping and torture charges against you, Mr. West. You and your sidekicks."

"File away. Just understand that if anything happens to Lorry Kennedy, otherwise known as Betty Sewell, or to Kevin Long, who is being held hostage by Robert's New York syndicate, then we'll take a pound of Robert's flesh. Pound by pound. We'll slice him up in ways you don't want to imagine. So tell Antonio that. And tell him if he has any sway with the men holding Kevin or tracking Lorry, he'd better get them in line."

"My client doesn't have a clue what you're talking about," Lumet said in a cold, dead voice.

Lucas noticed that Familiar had eased over to Robert. He was actually rubbing against the man's legs, as if they were friends. He pointed at the cat.

Familiar yawned, stood on his back legs and put his paws on Robert's knees. He only had to look into the gangster's eyes and Robert began to scream.

"Hey, and we aren't hurting him. We really aren't," Lucas said. "He's just a little gun-shy, I suppose."

"Antonio is not happy, Mr. West. You have no authority to hold Robert, and you certainly have no right to harm him."

"I want Kevin Long. I want him on the phone to me and then on a plane to Mobile, Alabama. When that's a done deal, say by early afternoon, then we'll talk about keeping Robert safe."

"You won't get away with this."

"Oh, I expect we'll get away with this and a whole lot more, Mr. Lumet. As you pointed out, I'm no longer held in check by the honor and integrity of the U.S. marshals. I'm a free agent. Your client shot my brother in cold blood. Don't you see a bit of Biblical destiny here? An eye for an eye. A tooth for a tooth. A brother for a brother." He ground out the last words. "Tell Kevin to call this number after he's boarded the plane."

"You'll release Robert then?"

"Call off your dogs. Get them off Lorry Kennedy's trail."

"You're going to regret crossing swords with the Maxims."

"No, Mr. Lumet, it's you who will live with regrets. You serve men who are evil and cruel. You know the money they pay you is acquired through the blood and suffering of young women whose only fault is that they have a dream. They want to be somebody. The Maxim organization turns them into drug addicts and prostitutes. That's where your money comes from. Enjoy it now, because one day you'll be paying the price."

Lucas softly closed the cell phone. Michelle was deathly pale. Even Greg had a furrow between his eyebrows.

"What?" Lucas asked.

"You really like to tease the lion, don't you?" Greg said.

"I'm hoping to prompt them to action," Lucas replied. He turned to Familiar. "Excellent work. You're the partner every lawman dreams of working with."

His comment broke the tension that had collected around the table. Michelle stood and gathered up the dishes. "I never thought I'd say that I looked forward to doing the dishes, but it actually sounds pleasant. Safe and humdrum and…pleasant."

WITH HER HANDS SOAKING in the hot water, Michelle hurriedly washed the plates and silverware and set them in the drain board. The hot water was a soothing influence as she let her thoughts drift back to the hour she'd shared with Lucas.

Desire, mingled with a hefty dose of fear and uncertainty, made her bite her lower lip. Lucas had chipped away the foundation she'd worked so hard to build—one that kept her feelings safely buried. Now she was experiencing a tidal surge of emotions.

The key element was joy. She'd never known what it felt like to truly share with another human, but she did now. And she wanted more. Whatever it took, she wanted to spend more time with Lucas. They were so different, their lives thousands of miles apart. But it didn't matter. Nothing mattered when she remembered his kisses or the way his hands had moved down her body, stirring feelings she'd never experienced before.

"Me-ow." Familiar brushed against her leg, winding around it and purring so loudly, she could hear it.

"Just one second." She finished the dishes and drained the sink, then tidied up the counters and stove top. When the chore was done, she sat at the table and pulled Familiar into her lap. "I owe you a lot," she said. "For so many things. Let's just say, I'll never be able to repay you for all you've done. But I want to do that series of photographs. I'll make a copy for you. A gift."

She brushed the top of his head, and he purred even louder. Both front paws came up and captured her hand.

"What?" she asked.

"Me-ow." Familiar went to the garbage can that held old newspapers and managed to pull one out. "Meow!" he insisted as he tapped his paw against the paper.

Michelle knelt down beside him, examining the paper. Maybe they'd missed a news story about something important. Instead, she found that she was looking at the Classified section.

Familiar batted the page, and she turned it. His black paw centered on Lost and Found. Curious, she read the several notices about pets missing or pets found, purses left behind and some Good Samaritan who'd found cash and wanted to return it to the proper owners. *Amazing*.

"What am I looking for?" she asked the cat.

He pawed an ad about a found pet; she read it carefully but still didn't understand.

Familiar got the camera she'd bought. He brought it to her and then went and stood in front of the lens.

When she saw that, he went back to the newspaper and patted the found-pet ad.

When she caught on to what he wanted, she almost squealed with pleasure.

"Lucas, Greg, come here. Familiar has a brilliant idea," she said.

The two men came into the kitchen. Lucas touched her shoulder as he passed, and heat sizzled through her, but she ignored it.

"Look," she said, pointing to the ads. "We can run an ad in the newspaper about a found cat. We can call him Familiar, and we can use a photo of him. We can place this ad in the newspaper with a phone number. When Lorry sees it, she'll call in! This was all Familiar's idea."

Lucas nodded. "It's a good one, too, assuming Lorry is still in this area."

Michelle felt her bubble burst. Lorry could

be in Hawaii by now. But as soon as her hopes fell, she felt them rise. "I believe she's close, Lucas."

"Why do you believe that?" he asked gently.

"Where would she go? She's safest in a part of the world she knows intimately. She could hide here for the next ten years. She's got friends to help her, and this is her home."

Lucas nodded. Michelle could tell she was getting to him, making sense.

"And what will it hurt to run the ad?" she said. "Lorry will recognize Familiar, and the Maxim minions will never think to look in the classifieds, under lost and found pets."

"You got a point there," Greg agreed.

"Let's give it a shot," Lucas said. "I'm ready to hear that Kevin is on a plane and that Lorry is safe. Let's see if we can make both of those things happen."

Chapter Nineteen

Michelle scanned the lost-and-found section of the Mobile *Press-Register* and quickly found the photograph of Familiar, looking pitiful and lost. She'd e-mailed the photograph and ad content to the paper Wednesday morning. Now, she read the ad with grim satisfaction. If Lorry/Betty was checking, which Lucas had prearranged with her in case of trouble, she'd get the message clearly. Lorry would certainly remember Familiar from the wedding. Who could forget the black cat swiping food from the buffet table?

Michelle put the paper aside and began preparations for breakfast. The night had passed in a state of bliss. She and Lucas had made love until exhausted, and they'd fallen asleep holding each other. Each moment had been precious.

Even as she cooked the bacon that Greg had

purchased at a store nearby, she couldn't dispel the sense that time was slipping away from them. It was Thursday morning. They had so little time to find Lorry and get her to New York if she was going to testify against Antonio Maxim.

If Lorry didn't testify, a murderer would walk free. And Kevin would die. And she and Lucas and Lorry would be hunted and killed without mercy.

She took a cup of coffee to Robert and uncuffed one hand while he drank it. She stood ten feet away, Greg's gun at the ready. Funny, but while she understood Robert was a dangerous and ruthless criminal, she was no longer afraid of him.

Robert eyed her speculatively as he sipped the coffee. As long as Familiar wasn't in the room, he acted the tough guy. The cat, though, could make him scream simply by walking past him.

"Look at you," Robert said softly. "Holding a gun on an unarmed man. You're a kidnapper, a torturer. A week ago you were the toast of SoHo as a photographer." He chuckled to himself. "What a comedown." He paused dramatically. "But I can change all of that. I can make it disappear. I can give you a new identity and enough money to set up your photography business in Paris or Rome."

"And you'd do that for me? Why?" She knew the answer, and beneath her calm questions, she felt a surge of anger that Robert thought he could manipulate her so easily.

"Because you let me go. If you'll put the gun down and unlock this other handcuff—"

"You'll forget all the things I've done."

He nodded. "Not only forget, but give you enough money so that you can forget, too."

She shrugged a shoulder. "How much?"

He studied her intensely. "Half a million. Cash. Transferred into a Cayman account. No questions asked. Give me the telephone, and I'll do it now."

"What about Lucas and Greg? And Kevin?"

"Kevin will be released. He knows nothing of value. The U.S. marshal…" His face tightened into a mask of hatred. "He will pay. He has to. The other one." He shrugged. "He dies, too."

"You are something," Michelle said softly. "You think I'd betray these two good men for money?"

Robert merely stared at her. "A million, then."

She used the barrel of the gun to indicate the floor. "Put the coffee cup down, and scoot it to me with your foot."

"I can make you wealthy and famous."

"And I can make you dead." She leveled the gun. "Not everyone in the world can be bought, Mr. Maxim. Ponder that while you rot in prison."

She picked up the coffee cup and stepped back. "Lucas!"

He appeared in the hallway, his shirt and hair rum-pled and a shy grin on his face. "Yes, ma'am?"

Michelle thought her heart would leap from her chest. Looking at him brought back every intimate second of the previous night, and she forced a gruffness into her voice that belied the heat that touched her cheeks. "Hook him back up. He's had his coffee. Maybe Familiar will feed him breakfast."

Lucas looked at her. "What's got you so hot under the collar?"

"Interacting with scum, I guess. We'll talk later." She went back to the kitchen and began preparing eggs. When Lucas entered, she gave him the newspaper and watched the smile spread across his face.

"If Lorry is in the area, she'll respond to that. She knows to check this paper online, too. She'll call. Especially since the number listed is her home phone. That was an ingenious idea, Michelle. And putting in there that Friday is the deadline before the cat will be sent to a shelter was so smart. Lorry can read between the lines. She'll know exactly what that means. I'm sure she'll call us." He walked over to her and pulled her against him. His lips warmed her neck.

Shivers danced down her body, and she almost dropped the spatula. "Keep that up, and no one will eat breakfast this morning."

"Who needs food when—"

"Me-ow!" Familiar's protest was loud and clear.

Michelle eased away from Lucas. "He needs food, and he needs it now."

"He's smart and all of that, but he's sure a demanding little fella." Lucas barely got the words from his mouth when Familiar darted across the floor and sank his teeth into Lucas's shin.

Michelle couldn't help herself. She laughed out loud as Lucas danced around, trying to dislodge the cat, who had now gotten his claws into the act.

"Okay, okay, you get breakfast. Anything you want!" Lucas finally stood still, and Familiar dropped to the floor and began to groom himself.

"I guess you see who's running this show," Michelle said as she kissed Lucas's cheek. "And don't mess with the boss man. He may be short of stature, but he's got one heck of a set of choppers."

"I got it this time." Lucas got a stack of plates and began to help Michelle prepare the food.

THE MOOD AROUND THE KITCHEN is all lovey-dovey, which I'm glad to see, don't get me wrong, but we're a long way from the finish line on this case. If Lorry doesn't call, or if Lucas doesn't find her, then we're in big, big trouble. Lucas, Michelle and Greg could be facing prison terms for kidnapping. If Antonio is freed, the Maxims will spare nothing to get even with Miss Shutterbug and Marshal West.

But it won't hurt to have one good meal that's relaxed and pleasant. And Lucas will make some calls to the Austin office and see if they've heard from Lorry. I'm worried about her, but I know she's smart and a survivor.

I have to trust that she's doing okay, watching and waiting for the right moment to reveal herself.

Lucas and Michelle are both forcing themselves to look on the bright side—that Lorry will see the ad and get in touch in time to get a flight to New York.

My concern is that she's far away. Far enough gone that she can't get back by tomorrow. I mean, her cover was blown, and people were shooting at her with automatic weapons. I think I'd take a powder, too.

But it's only 7:00 a.m., and I'm not going to become anxious until noon. Right now, I'm going to eat that crisp bacon and enjoy a cheese and egg omelet.

I hear Greg stirring. The smell of the bacon must have awakened him. Robert is being a good boy. I just checked on him. In fact, he's being really good. That makes me worry. But I'll attend to him after breakfast. Maybe a thirty-minute session of staring at his shins. Or his inner thighs. Ye-ow! That's a tender spot, and if I so much as look at him, he gets all nervous.

But right now, time for grub.

LUCAS PUSHED HIS PLATE back and sighed. "That was delicious, Michelle."

"I second that." Greg patted his stomach. "I may need a nap."

"Thanks." Michelle rose and began to stack the dishes, but Lucas stopped her. "The cook rests. Greg and I can do this."

"Wow," Michelle said, grinning. "A sensitive cowboy-marshal-kidnapper. And I thought that wasn't possible."

"Tease all you want," Lucas said as he cleared the table. "My mom cooked for the family and twenty hands. We all pitched in to help her. Harry and I—" He broke off and cleared his throat.

"Harry spoke about the farm all the time," Greg said softly. "I think he was about ready to give up law enforcement and go back to the land. He missed it a lot. He would be proud that you're ranching, Lucas."

"Yeah. I think he would," Lucas concurred.

He was about to say something else when he heard the ringing of a phone. They all froze.

"It's my cell phone," Michelle said, rushing to grab it. She checked the caller ID. "I don't know this number."

"Answer it," Lucas said.

She answered with a calm hello. Her face broke into the widest smile. "Kevin! Where are you?" She looked at Lucas. "He's on a flight to Mobile. They're about to take off."

Lucas put a hand on her shoulder. "Good news." His wide smile told her how happy he was that her friend was safe.

"Kevin, call us when you land. We'll make arrangements to pick you up. Thank goodness you're okay," she said before she ended the conversation.

"That video you made worked," Greg said. He, too, was smiling.

Lucas glanced at both of them. "Now to find

Lorry. I'm going to make some calls to the Austin office to see if anyone there has heard anything from her."

He picked up his cell phone and dialed Frank Holcomb's number. If anyone had news of Lorry, it would be his old partner. But he also knew that Frank would have called him if there was news.

The phone rang and rang, and Lucas felt a sense of unease. When at last someone answered, he didn't recognize the voice.

"Where's Frank?" Lucas asked.

"Who's asking?"

Lucas identified himself and then heard a muffled conversation on the other end. A different voice came back on. "Frank didn't report in this morning. We're trying to track him down."

"Captain Wells?" Lucas asked.

"We're worried about Frank, Lucas. He left work yesterday and headed to New York. He got a call from the NYPD, saying they had a lead. We were hoping the witness might show up there. I have to tell you. Frank said that whatever else happened, Antonio would not walk out of that courthouse a free man."

Lucas didn't have to ask what Frank had meant. He knew. The marshal was willing to destroy his future to make certain Antonio wasn't out on the street to continue destroying young women. "Any word from the witness?" Lucas asked, though he knew the answer.

"Nothing. But the appeal has been postponed until tomorrow."

"I'll find her."

"I sure hope you can," Wells said. "Without Lorry, the state has nothing."

MICHELLE CHECKED HER WATCH and paced some more. The morning had slipped away from them. The afternoon had crept by. It was nearly 4:00 p.m. They were due to pick up Kevin at the airport in another hour.

And no word from Lorry.

Throughout the day, Robert Maxim's smile had widened and widened. Now he looked like a hungry carnivore. And she felt like steak. She'd retreated to the kitchen, where she could keep an eye on the telephone. If wishing something could make it true, the phone would ring and Lorry would be on the other end, safe and sound.

Lucas had been huddled with Greg outside, but he came in and put an arm around her. "We've done everything I know to do, Michelle."

"When's the last flight out of Mobile?" she asked.

"At eight tonight."

"If you and Lorry miss that flight, Antonio will be a free man by this time tomorrow." She sighed. "What will we do with Robert?"

"I don't know."

She could see that Lucas didn't have any answers, either. "Where can Lorry be?" she asked.

"Me-ow!" Familiar leaped to the kitchen table and then to the window over the sink, which looked out on the sloping yard. "Me-ow!" He battered the window with his body.

"What's wrong with him?" Michelle asked. She'd been staring out the window only a few minutes before, but the cat was acting as if someone were outside.

Lucas gripped the gun he'd taken from Robert Maxim and held it. He stepped in front of Michelle, protecting her.

She looked around him and couldn't stop the sudden intake of breath. Someone was standing in the yard. A solitary person was there, staring at the house.

"Who the hell is that?" she asked.

"I don't know, but I'm going to find out." Lucas started toward the back door, but Familiar was out of it like a shot. The black cat rushed across the lawn, making a beeline for the solitary figure.

Michelle watched from the window, her heart pounding, as the cat and the man began to run toward the figure. She knew who it was. She knew.

As the woman stepped out of the shadows and into the sunlight, Michelle clearly saw Lorry Kennedy. She bent to sweep the cat into her arms, and in a moment Lucas had both of them in his.

Michelle gripped the sink and waited. This was a moment she'd never forget. She owed Lorry an apology. More than an apology. How was she ever going to make things right?

Lucas, Lorry and Familiar walked toward the house. Michelle dried her hands and turned to face the door. When Lorry stepped through, Michelle saw the worry etched into her face, the fear.

"I'm so sorry," she said.

Lorry's face softened, and Michelle could see the planes and angles that had made her wedding photograph so extraordinary. "Lucas explained how it happened. You couldn't have known."

Michelle blinked back the tears. "Where's your husband?"

"Safe. We're both going to be safe now."

"We need to get to the airport," Lucas said. "I have to get Lorry to New York."

"I'm going, too," Michelle said. There was no way she'd stay behind.

"Me-ow."

Lucas looked from one to the other. "Greg can stay here with Robert Maxim."

"Robert." Lorry's smile faltered. "He's here."

"The less you know, the better," Lucas said. "We'll grab some clothes and be ready to leave in five minutes. Let me talk to Greg. When Kevin gets here, he can help Greg with our...guest."

"I'll be ready in less than five minutes." Michelle didn't care about anything but getting on the airplane with Lucas and getting Lorry safely to the courtroom.

"They'll be expecting us in New York," Lucas said quietly. "My old partner is there. Frank will help us."

"We're going to need all the help we can get," Lorry said. "If there was ever a time to bring out the big guns, it's now."

Chapter Twenty

Michelle leaned back in the seat as the plane rumbled down the runway. She clutched the armrest, remembering how haggard Kevin had looked. He'd stepped off the plane, lost and frightened. In the few minutes they'd had together in the Mobile airport, Kevin had assured her that he hadn't been mistreated. He'd been fed and given water, and no one had struck him. But they had threatened him repeatedly.

All in all, though, he'd assured her he was fine, and he'd been more than willing to drive to Spanish Fort and help Greg watch over Robert Maxim.

He'd driven away into the night, leaving Michelle and Lucas and Lorry to board their flight to New York.

Although she was afraid of what would await them in the city, Michelle focused on the fact that both Kevin and Lorry were alive and unharmed. So far.

The Maxim organization would no doubt attempt to thwart Lorry from getting to the courthouse to testify. And so far, Lucas had been unable to contact his ex-partner, Frank Holcomb. It was as if the U.S. marshal had disappeared from the planet.

Lucas wasn't saying anything, but Michelle knew him well enough to know that he was very worried. She slipped her hand into his, and he squeezed. He sat between her and Lorry and Familiar was in Lorry's lap, looking out the window as the plane jetted through the night sky.

Michelle glanced at Lucas, glad to see that his eyes were shut. She hoped that he was sleeping. They'd made their plans, covering every angle possible. As soon as they disembarked at LaGuardia, they would maneuver through the airport until they were certain no one was tailing them. A hired limo would whisk them out of the airport.

Lucas had booked rooms under a different name at a hotel close to the courtroom where Antonio Maxim's appeal would be heard.

In the morning, when they got inside the courtroom, the worst would be over.

She checked her watch. It was 8:45 p.m.

Another three hours and they'd be in the Big Apple. Until then, all she could do was cling to Lucas's hand and let him know that whatever happened, they were in it together.

I'VE GIVEN THIS A LOT of thought, and I think it should be mandatory that bad guys wear black hats. In all the westerns I've watched, it makes the criminals a lot easier to keep up with. While we know what Robert and Antonio Maxim look like, we have no idea who's working for them. We can't pick them out of a crowd or tell if one of them is the limo driver. They appear to be ordinary people. And that's dangerous.

There's no other way this could go down, but the idea of walking into LaGuardia, a sitting duck for one of the Maxim henchmen to use for target practice—that just doesn't sit well with me.

But we have to get to the city, and Lorry has to testify. The plane was the only choice. There's no other way to get there on time. The problem is, they're bound to be watching the airports. Lucas thought about flying into Newark or some other close-by place and driving into the city, but time is against us, and there's every chance the Maxims are watching every airport in the area.

We are traveling under assumed names. It

was easy enough for Lucas's old boss to arrange that small detail, but Lorry, Lucas and Michelle are all easily identifiable. Unlike the criminal humanoids.

I'll just have to keep my eagle eyes open and protect Miss Shutterbug and Cowboy Marshal. And Lorry, too. She's been through hell, but she's determined to put Antonio away. I was afraid that after all that's happened, she might not want to testify. I gravely misjudged her. She's got character and inner strength.

I'm always giving bipeds a hard time, but then I meet someone like Lorry, who has given up so much to do the right thing. And Michelle. She's done everything she can to make up for her mistake.

Ah, this is a hard case, but I have to say, I enjoy traveling in the company of two beautiful broads. Not even James Bond had it this good.

Now for a little shut-eye. We'll be in the Big Apple before long, and there won't be time for sleeping. I'm never at my best when I'm sleep deprived. No feline is. So I'll snooze while the snoozing is good.

THE LANDING GEAR ENGAGED, and Lucas woke abruptly from his light sleep. It was almost midnight, a time he'd been terrified of as a young child. This was the hour between day and night, the time when monsters roamed. Those were childhood fears and fancies, and he'd put them behind him long ago. This midnight, though, was one of extreme danger. Not from monsters that hid beneath the bed, but from bad men with deadly guns. Men who would murder for money.

He glanced over at Familiar, who'd sprawled across Michelle's lap. The cat stared deep into his eyes, and he felt as if the feline were offering reassurance.

"Thank you," he whispered.

The cat nodded.

Lucas felt a surge of hope. With Familiar, it was possible they could avoid the Maxim organization and that Lorry would testify safely in less than ten hours.

He looked at the young woman who had willingly risked her life to bring his brother's killer to justice. And at the red-haired photographer on his left. They were courageous. Not fearless, but truly brave. He'd learned long ago that courage was not the act of being fearless, but taking action even when one was afraid.

He silently vowed to keep them safe or die trying. Lorry had had a week of hell, moving from one low-rent motel to another, always in the South Alabama area, always checking the newspaper to see if she should make contact.

Always afraid that someone would recognize her and kill her or Charles.

At least she'd convinced her husband to stay in Spanish Fort and help Greg and Kevin guard Robert Maxim. Michelle should have stayed. God knows he'd tried to convince her, but along with her fiery temper, she was as hard-headed as a...well, as a West.

"Why are you grinning?" Michelle asked.

He didn't know how long she'd been watching him, but his smile widened. "Thinking about how bullheaded you are. It occurred to me that I've got a young mare you need to meet. I think she can match you pound for pound in the area of stubbornness. I could take bets to see which one would last the longest."

"Very funny." She sat up and adjusted Familiar in her lap.

The captain's voice came on, telling them that landing was imminent. Lorry, too, opened her eyes. "Lucas thinks he's the only one who isn't stubborn. In his head, he's well reasoned or sensible or just plain right. He's never stubborn."

"No fair ganging up on me," he protested.

Before he could add anything, Familiar put a paw on his mouth. "Me-ow."

Both women laughed. "Even the cat is telling you that you're stubborn," Michelle said. "But it's okay, Lucas. We love you, anyway."

He saw the flush touch her cheeks as soon as the words were out of her mouth, and he leaned over and kissed her warm skin. "I love you, too," he whispered.

The furious color deepened, and Lorry arched an eyebrow. "Lucas West, you devil. You've gone and fallen in love, haven't you?"

Lucas felt his own skin flush. "No sense in denying it. I have."

Lorry reached across him and grasped Michelle's hand. She picked up one of Lucas's calloused ones. "Something good has come from all this mess, Lucas. Remember that. We've all lost a lot to the Maxims. All of us. Especially you. But you've received something wonderful, too. Love is a gift."

Lucas was spared an answer when the wheels touched down, and the roar of the plane increased as it braked and began to slow.

According to the plan, Lorry hurried out of her seat and pushed her way out the door first. Lucas reasoned that no one would expect her to slip out alone. Next, he sent Michelle and Familiar. Lucas was only a few people behind them.

A few slow people. An older man dropped his bag and got it stuck between the seats. Lucas tried to help him, but with the press of passengers behind, the area became more congested. At last, Lucas freed the bag, and the disembarking passengers flowed into the tunnel and then the gateway.

He saw Familiar instantly. The cat's attention was locked down the concourse. And he saw why. Two men had taken up position on either side of Lorry. She put on a burst of speed, but they followed.

"Familiar!" The cat was his only hope.

As soon as the cat got into the gate area, he zeroed in on a young man hustling along and deliberately tripped him, sending him facedown in front of one of the would-be abductors.

Familiar never slowed. He darted out in front of a fast-moving tram, causing the driver to swerve and run into a coffee-shop area jammed with waiting passengers.

In less than thirty seconds, the gate area and concourse were in total pandemonium.

Hurrying down the hall, Lucas spotted Lorry running hard. Michelle was right behind her, checking left and right to make certain no one was following Lorry.

Familiar was a blur as he streaked out of the

coffee-shop fiasco and leaped onto the tables of a small eatery. Customers fell backward out of their chairs, food went flying. A hot coffee went directly into the face of Lorry's second pursuer. He grabbed his eyes and began yelling.

Lucas had to hand it to the cat. When Familiar agreed to create chaos, he did it with a flare that couldn't be matched. The cat was a tornado of destruction in the airport. Lucas hurried past a shrieking café manager with a broom and followed Lorry and Michelle.

When he glanced back, Familiar had eluded the manager and was hot on his heels. He stopped, bent down and scooped the cat into his arms. "Good work," he whispered.

Familiar's answer was a swipe of his sandpapery tongue across Lucas's jaw.

He caught up with the two women at the main door.

Instead of arranging the limo to pick them up at the baggage claim, he had the car pick them up at the front of the airline terminal.

Lucas stepped into the night and flicked a cigarette lighter three times. A long black limo answered by hitting its bright lights.

"There's the car." With Familiar still in his arms and a woman on either side, he ran across the line of vehicles putting out passengers.

They dove into the limo amidst a shrill of whistles from the airport authorities.

"Floor it," Lucas ordered the driver.

The man complied, and they shot into traffic and away from the airport. At last, Lucas exhaled. He felt as if he'd been holding his breath for an hour. As they merged into the flow of traffic in the town that never slept, he glanced at Michelle and Lorry. The strain was evident in their faces, but so was the pride. They'd gotten out of the airport without injury or a tail.

"Cancel the trip to the hotel," Lucas said to the driver. "Take us straight to Saint Patrick's Cathedral."

"It's closed," the driver said, looking over his shoulder at them as if they were nuts.

"A refuge from evil is never closed," Lucas answered.

"Me-ow," Familiar chimed in.

MICHELLE INHALED SHARPLY when she saw Lucas wearing the robes of a Catholic priest. Tall, slender, his gray eyes blazing and serious, he looked the part. And in the early morning light, Lorry, in the garb of a nun, looked equally perfect.

"Thank you, Father," Lucas said to the priest.

"Bring the habit and the robes back without

any holes in them." The priest's tone was serious, but he backed it up with a smile.

"We'll do our best," replied Lucas.

The priest patted Lorry's arm. "The Maxims have destroyed the lives of hundreds of young girls. Sometimes we get a few of the lucky ones, those who haven't surrendered to the drugs. We help them heal, give them funds to start a new life. But they can never recover what was stolen from them. Their youth, their innocence, their trust in a dream. That's gone forever. The Maxims are evil men. I hope you send both of them to prison for a long, long time."

"I hope so, too, Father," Lucas said. "Thank you for your help with this." He glanced at his watch. "Now it's time to go."

Outside, the streets were busy with the workday bustle of a large city. Michelle picked up Familiar and put him on the sofa in the large anteroom. Lucas had ordered her to remain in the church, with Familiar, where they were both safe. She swallowed the bitter lump of disappointment. He was putting her safety first, but still, it felt as if she'd come on a long journey just to be shut out at the end.

"We're going to get to the courthouse early," Lucas said. "Once we're inside, I think we'll be safe."

"Be careful," she whispered. His arms encircled her, and he kissed her long and hard and with such passion that she forgot everything except the love she felt for him.

When he broke the kiss, he turned and left. Lorry was waiting at the door. They stepped outside, and the heavy door closed with a booming echo.

Lucas had been gone barely a minute when she felt Familiar brushing her legs. He hooked her pants with his sharp claws and began urging her toward the door.

"Oh, no," she said. "I gave Lucas my word."

"Me-ow!" Familiar insisted. He tugged at her pants leg with this claws.

"If we show up, he'll only have to worry about protecting us as well as Lorry." Even as she said the words, she knew Familiar wasn't going to listen. "And Lucas thinks I'm hard-headed," she said out loud.

The cat hopped up in a window and pushed at a small crack. In a matter of moments, he'd made an exit large enough to slip through.

"Familiar!" She ran after him. "I'll be back, Father," she called out as she grabbed a shawl from the coatrack beside the door. "Thank you!" And then she was out the door. The cat had somehow managed to flag a taxi. He was leaping into a window when she grabbed the door handle and managed to get inside.

"Take us to the courthouse," she said. One impulsive, high-handed act had gotten her into a mess that had nearly cost several people their lives. She could only hope that she wasn't making the same mistake twice.

Chapter Twenty-One

Michelle draped the shawl over her red hair and joined the men and women headed into the courthouse. Familiar was hidden in the folds of the shawl. She'd never been inside this building. Never anticipated that one day she'd be there, except maybe for jury duty.

She put Familiar down before she went through the security check. The cat was smart enough to figure a way inside on his own. He'd probably beat her to the courtroom.

She stopped and asked a deputy where to find the Maxim appeal, and she was following his directions when she saw Lorry and Lucas. They were moving silently along the hallway toward the courtroom.

She took a deep breath. Lucas was going to be furious, and justifiably so. She dropped back, easing behind several men. Familiar was out of sight, but she had no doubt the cat was fine.

Lucas and Lorry had stopped at the court-room doors. She fell back behind another man, hoping they'd enter so she could slip in the rear.

The man in front of her reached into his coat. The movement was so smooth, so practiced. Michelle didn't register what it meant until she saw the gun. The man brought the weapon out and aimed it at Lorry's head.

Before she could even scream, Familiar came out of nowhere. He landed on the gunman's arm just as he squeezed off the bullet. There was the sound of a gunshot echoing off the marble walls as people shrieked and began to panic.

Lucas and Lorry turned, seemingly in slow motion. They were twenty feet away, and as Michelle watched in horror, the gunman lifted the gun again.

Lucas dove in front of Lorry, and Michelle kicked the gunman's arm. Everything seemed to take forever. She felt her toe connect with his elbow, and she saw him begin to fall. She heard the shot, she saw the gun fly from his hand, she turned to see blood spatter the wall behind Lucas, and she saw him begin to crumble. He fought to keep his feet, but he couldn't.

Lucas slumped to the floor, in Lorry's arms. Before the gunman could struggle to his feet,

Michelle kicked him in the ribs. Familiar jumped on his face, sharp claws tearing into the tender flesh.

The gunman began to scream, and a man in jeans and a sweatshirt flashed a U.S. marshal's badge and knelt on the gunman's chest. "I'm Frank Holcomb, Lucas's former partner. See how bad he's hurt."

Michelle ran to Lucas. Her hearing had blurred, so that everything sounded like an echo. She saw terrified people running, but her focus was on Lucas and the pool of blood that was seeping around Lorry.

She tore the shawl free and pressed it into the wound in Lucas's shoulder. "Pressure," she told Lorry. "We have to keep pressure on it."

Frank appeared and pressed his hands on top of hers. "He's going to be okay. He has to."

Until the paramedics came to pull her away, she fought to staunch the flow of blood from Lucas's wound. As the paramedics began to load Lucas onto a gurney, he grasped Michelle's hand. "Stay with Lorry," he said. "You and Familiar."

THE COURTROOM WAS HUSHED as Lorry took the stand. In a matter of minutes, the prosecutor walked her through her testimony. She pointed at Antonio Maxim, identifying him as the gunman who shot and killed Harry West. There was no hesitation. And none when the judge denied Antonio's appeal and returned him to a life in prison without parole.

LUCAS SHIFTED IN THE hospital bed. It was ridiculous for them to keep him, but the doctor had refused to let him go. The bullet had gone through his shoulder, but there was no permanent damage.

"Hey, cowboy," Frank said. "You need to relax and heal."

"Easy for you to say," Lucas said.

Frank stood at the side of the bed. "Before your fan club arrives, I have to tell you something. NYPD found the mole, an officer the Maxims were squeezing hard to make him cooperate. They had his daughter. He's the one who betrayed Harry."

Lucas sighed. "I wish I felt vindication, but I don't. The Maxims have ruined countless lives."

"And now they'll be punished," Frank said. "It won't undo the past, but now they've been stopped."

The hospital door opened, and Michelle entered, carrying a large bag. Behind her, Lorry had a container that smelled suspiciously like hot pizza. Lucas felt a rush of relief, followed by unreasonable anger. Michelle could have been killed.

"You are the most stubborn woman I've ever met," he said.

"And thank goodness for that," Lorry said evenly. "She saved our lives, Lucas."

"Not really," Michelle said. She put the bag on the bed and opened it. Familiar eased out, arching his back and walking up to Lucas so that he could rub his whiskers against Lucas's face. "It was Familiar. He jumped on the gunman's arm."

"Maybe we should swear in Familiar *and* Michelle as marshals," Frank said. "They've got the grit."

"Don't encourage her," Lucas warned.

Michelle leaned over the bed and placed a gentle kiss on his lips. "I thought you were dying," she said. Tears filled her eyes.

That was more than Lucas could take. He wrapped his uninjured arm around her and pulled her close. "Thank god you weren't hurt."

"We're all fine," Lorry said. "And Antonio is behind bars, where he belongs. For life."

"What about Robert?" Lucas asked. He felt as if he'd been shut out of the main action. Everything had happened, and he'd been in an ambulance or in the emergency room.

"Greg turned him over to the Baldwin County sheriff," said Frank. "They're transporting him back to Dallas to face a long list of charges."

Michelle laughed. "Greg said Robert did his best to convince the sheriff that he'd been kidnapped, held hostage and tortured by a black cat. No one believed a word of it. They had a doctor check him over, and there were these teensy tiny little marks that might have been made by a cat's claws, but everyone laughed at the idea that those were marks of torture."

Lucas watched light play across Michelle's face as she spoke. She was the most beautiful woman he'd ever seen. And the smartest. And she was brave beyond reason.

Frank leaned a little closer so he could whisper. "Lucas, you're looking a little like a moonstruck calf."

At first Lucas almost denied it, but then he reached up to brush a strand of hair from Michelle's face. "Maybe so, partner, but if you were in my shoes, you'd be the luckiest man alive."

"When's the wedding?" Lorry asked. "This time I get to return the favor, and *I'll* take the photographs."

"I'll never live that down," Michelle said, but she put her arm around Lorry and hugged her.

"I'm not even sure this woman will have me for a husband," Lucas said. He couldn't look away from Michelle. He saw so many things in her eyes, including his future.

"You haven't really asked," Michelle said.

"You'll forgive me if I don't go down on bended knee. Or that I don't have a ring. Or that this setting isn't a high hill on my ranch, with the moon shining down and coyotes singing in the background. That's where I thought I might propose."

"None of that matters," Michelle said. Her eyes were bright with tears, but Lucas knew these were tears of happiness.

"Michelle Sieck, will you marry me?" he asked.

"I will, Lucas West." She leaned down and kissed him.

"What about your photography?" Lorry asked.

Michelle put her hand on Lucas's shoulder. "It's strange, but I've developed this yearning to capture the Hill Country of Texas on film. Somehow, I don't think I can get in trouble photographing cows."

Lucas joined in the laughter, but his thoughts were serious. He would make her happy. And he would spend the rest of his days making sure that she was safe.

AH, ANOTHER WEDDING LOOMS. Hopefully, this one will be simpler and without the drama of Lorry's. But Lucas and Michelle would never have found each other without all the events, both good and tragic, that came from Lorry's wedding. Now that's all behind them. Lucas should be out of the hospital by tomorrow, and he and Michelle will head to Texas. Lorry will return to Spanish Fort with Charles, and I'll go home to Washington and my splendid Clotilde.

Eleanor and Peter will be glad to see me, though I understand they're planning some sort of trip to South Dakota. Geez, I'm not sure I'm up for another vacation. Somehow, those things always end up with a beautiful woman, a puzzle and danger.

For the moment, I'll think only about my homecoming. My pillow in the window beside the garden; Clotilde coming through the daffodils to pay me a visit; Eleanor in the kitchen, whipping up something sumptuous and tantalizing just for me. I wonder what she'll serve. Every time I come home from an adventure, Eleanor creates the most exotic and wonderful dishes. Something with fish, of course. Perhaps some of that grilled salmon that I adore.

Goodness, I'm drooling on the hospital sheets. And the bipeds are laughing at me. Well, let them have their pleasure. Familiar, black cat detective, was on the spot when he was needed. Another chapter for my memoirs.

* * * * *

*Don't miss the next
Fear Familiar adventure,
FAMILIAR SHOWDOWN,
available in August 2009!
Only from Caroline Burnes
and Harlequin Intrigue.*

'I've found her.'

Max froze.

It was what he'd been waiting for since June, but now—now he was almost afraid to voice the question. His heart stalling, he leaned slowly back in his chair and scoured the investigator's face for clues. 'Where?' he asked, and his voice sounded rough and unused, like a rusty hinge.

'In Suffolk. She's living in a cottage.'

Living. His heart crashed back to life, and he sucked in a long, slow breath. All these months he'd feared—

'Is she well?'

'Yes, she's well.'

He had to force himself to ask the next question. 'Alone?'

The man paused. 'No. The cottage belongs to a man called John Blake. He's working away at the moment, but he comes and goes.'

God. He felt sick. So sick he hardly registered the next few words, but then gradually
they sank in. 'She's got *what?*'

'Babies. Twin girls. They're eight months
old.'

'Eight—?' he echoed under his breath. 'They
must be his.'

He was thinking out loud, but the P.I. heard
and corrected him.

'Apparently not. I gather they're hers. She's
been there since mid-January last year, and they
were born during the summer—June, the
woman in the post office thought. She was
more than helpful. I think there's been a certain
amount of speculation about their relationship.'

He'd just bet there had. God, he was going
to kill her. Or Blake. Maybe both of them.

'Of course, looking at the dates, she was pre-
sumably pregnant when she left you, so they
could be yours, or she could have been having
an affair with this Blake character before…'

He glared at the unfortunate P.I. 'Just stick
to your job. I can do the math,' he snapped,
swallowing the unpalatable possibility that
she'd been unfaithful to him before she'd left.
'Where is she? I want the address.'

'It's all in here,' the man said, sliding a
large envelope across the desk to him. 'With
my invoice.'

'I'll get it seen to. Thank you.'

'If there's anything else you need, Mr Gallagher, any further information—'

'I'll be in touch.'

'The woman in the post office told me Blake was away at the moment, if that helps,' he added quietly, and opened the door.

Max stared down at the envelope, hardly daring to open it, but when the door clicked softly shut behind the P.I., he eased up the flap, tipped it and felt his breath jam in his throat as the photos spilled out over the desk.

Oh, lord, she looked gorgeous. Different, though. It took him a moment to recognise her, because she'd grown her hair, and it was tied back in a ponytail, making her look younger and somehow freer. The blond highlights were gone, and it was back to its natural soft golden-brown, with a little curl in the end of the ponytail that he wanted to thread his finger through and tug, just gently, to draw her back to him.

Crazy. She'd put on a little weight, but it suited her. She looked well and happy and beautiful, but oddly, considering how desperate he'd been for news of her for the past year—one year, three weeks and two days, to be exact—it wasn't only Julia who held his attention after the initial shock. It was the babies sitting side by side in a supermarket trolley. Two identical and absolutely beautiful little girls.

* * * * *

When Max Gallagher hires a P.I. to find his estranged wife, Julia, he discovers she's not alone—she has twin baby girls, and they might be his. Now workaholic Max has just two weeks to prove that he can be a wonderful husband and father to the family he wants to treasure.

Look for
TWO LITTLE MIRACLES
by Caroline Anderson,
available February 2009
from Harlequin Romance®

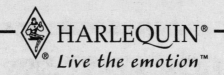

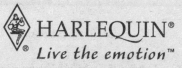

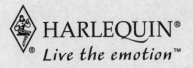

HARLEQUIN®
SuperRomance®

...there's more to the story!

Superromance.
A *big* satisfying read about unforgettable
characters. Each month we offer *six* very different
stories that range from family drama to adventure
and mystery, from highly emotional stories to
romantic comedies—and much more! Stories
about people you'll believe in and care about.
Stories too compelling to put down....

Our authors are among today's *best* romance
writers. You'll find familiar names and talented
newcomers. Many of them are award winners—
and you'll see why!

If you want the biggest and best
in romance fiction, you'll get it
from Superromance!

Exciting, Emotional, Unexpected...

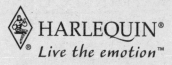

HARLEQUIN®
Live the emotion™

HARLEQUIN®
Presents®

The world's bestselling romance series...
The series that brings you your favorite authors,
month after month:

Helen Bianchin...Emma Darcy
Lynne Graham...Penny Jordan
Miranda Lee...Sandra Marton
Anne Mather...Carole Mortimer
Melanie Milburne...Michelle Reid

and many more talented authors!

Wealthy, powerful, gorgeous men...
Women who have feelings just like your own...
The stories you love, set in exotic, glamorous locations...

HARLEQUIN®
Presents®

Seduction and Passion Guaranteed!

HPDIR08

Harlequin® Historical
Historical Romantic Adventure!

*Imagine a time of chivalrous
knights and unconventional ladies,
roguish rakes and impetuous
heiresses, rugged cowboys
and spirited frontierswomen—
these rich and vivid tales will
capture your imagination!*

*Harlequin Historical . . .
they're too good to miss!*